The Magic Mirror

and
Other Stories

by
ENID BLYTON

Illustrated by
Mike Taylor

AWARD PUBLICATIONS LIMITED

For further information on Enid Blyton please contact
www.blyton.com

ISBN 0-86163-931-6

First published 1998
4th impression 2001

Published by Award Publications Limited,
27 Longford Street, London NW1 3DZ

Printed in Singapore

CONTENTS

The Magic Mirror   5
The Boy With a Thousand Wishes   15
The Thrush and His Anvil   30
The Foolish White Horse   36
Happy New Year!   46
The Secret Garden   55
One Rainy Night   73
The Lost Doll's Pram   82
Clever Mr Trusty   93
It's Really True!   102
Blue Shoes for the Party   111
The Mysterious Thief   123
Clever-One the Imp   141
Tinkle's Party   151
The Poor Pink Pig   164
The Squeaky Doll   180
The Grumpy Goblins   187

The
Magic Mirror

"Sammy, don't frown like that!" said his mother. "It makes you look so ugly."

Sammy looked up. His mother thought he looked a very ugly little boy. His forehead was wrinkled like an old man's, and the corners of his mouth were turned down.

"I can't think why you are always frowning," said his mother. "You ought to be cheerful and good-tempered, not gloomy and snappy, as you so often are. I don't know what you will be like when you are grown up!"

"I shall be all right," said Sammy, crossly.

"You won't," said his mother. "You make your grown-up face while you are still a child, you know. I think you will be

5

an ugly, cross man! Do cheer up, Sammy, and smile a bit, and be kind and jolly, instead of such a little crosspatch."

Sammy didn't believe his mother when she said that children made the faces they would have when they were grown-up. He thought that was silly. But it wasn't. It was quite true.

One day he met Old Man Blue-Eyes. He was a strange old fellow, with eyes as blue as the sky, a jolly red face, and a mouth that was always smiling. Everyone liked Old Man Blue-Eyes. Sammy did, because he was so merry and bright.

"Hello, hello!" said Old Man Blue-Eyes,

stopping by Sammy. "Still the same old frown, still the same old sulky mouth! My word, you'll be an ugly old man one day!"

"My mother says that sort of thing too," said Sammy. "She says that children make their grown-up faces while they are still children. But they don't, do they?"

"Of course they do!" said Old Man Blue-Eyes. "Now, Sammy, you come home with me for a minute or two, and I'll let you have a look in my magic mirror. Then you'll see that what your mother says is true. You do make your own face!"

A magic mirror! That sounded marvellous. Sammy trotted along with Old Man Blue-Eyes, feeling excited. The old man took him into his neat and tidy little cottage, and pointed to a dark wall. A curious mirror shone there, perfectly round, set in a shining silver frame.

"Now you go and look at yourself there whilst I talk to you," said Old Man Blue-Eyes. "Go along. You'll see something strange."

So Sammy went and stood in front of the mirror. At first he could see nothing for there seemed to be a kind of moving mist in the glass. Then it cleared, and he saw his own face.

"Look at your face now," said Old Man Blue-Eyes. "It could be a nice face, for it has big brown eyes, a generous sort of mouth, a straight nose, and nice wavy hair round it."

That was true. Sammy might have been a nice-looking boy if he hadn't frowned and sulked so much. He stared at his own face, and the old man went on talking quietly and sadly.

"Now see that frown on your forehead – see the wrinkles it makes, and the nasty little straight lines between your eyes – look at your mouth, turned down in a sulky way – see how gloomy those nice brown eyes look! Now watch!"

A mist came into the magic mirror again and for a few moments Sammy could see nothing. Then it cleared and he had a shock. He was still looking at himself – but he was much older!

"Here we are again," said Old Man Blue-Eyes. "Ten years older – a big boy, growing up. Unpleasant fellow he looks, doesn't he?"

He did! He looked cross and unfriendly. Sammy didn't like the look of him at all.

"See those frown-wrinkles there?" said Old Man Blue-Eyes. "Worse than ever, aren't they? They make that boy look

9

quite old! And did you ever see such an
ugly mouth? I shouldn't think that boy
has any friends, would you?"

"No," said Sammy. "I don't much like
the look of him. It's me isn't it?"

Old Man Blue-Eyes didn't answer. A mist came into the mirror again, and Sammy stared hard. What was coming next?

It cleared away, and another face looked out. It was the face of a grown man. Sammy hated it. It was a hard miserable face, and the forehead was wrinkled all over.

"Look at those wrinkles and the little lines between the eyes, the ones we make when we frown hard," said Old Man Blue-Eyes. "Don't they make this man's face ugly? And look at his mouth – see

the lines that run from his nose to his chin, and make him look so hard and old! I think he is a nasty fellow, don't you agree?"

"I don't want to see any more," said Sammy, frightened, for the man was very like him. But the face faded in a new mist, and then, when the mist went, another face was there – the face of a cross, ugly, unhappy old man.

"Here we are again," said Old Man Blue-Eyes. "What a poor miserable, bad-tempered old fellow! He has no friends to love him, and he loves no one, not even a dog. How I do pity him, don't you?"

"Yes," said Sammy, in a low voice. "I don't want to be like that. This mirror frightens me! Old Man Blue-Eyes, the people in the mirror aren't really me when I'm grown-up, are they?"

"I'm afraid so," said Old Man Blue-Eyes, in a sad voice. "We make our own faces, and we make our own lives, happy or unhappy. Didn't you see the frown-wrinkles and the sulky lines in those faces – just the same as you have now?

Well, they grow of course. It's a pity, Sammy – you could be a nice little boy if you liked."

Sammy slipped away without a word. He was very upset. He simply couldn't grow up like that! But what was he going to do about it? He went to look into his own mirror at home.

"I'll just smile, and see if that makes me any different," he thought. So he smiled. And oh, what a nice-looking little boy he saw in the mirror, what a kind little child! His eyes creased at the corners and were merry and bright, his mouth turned up, his wrinkles went.

"I'm the sort of boy people would want to be friends with," thought Sammy, in surprise. "I'm not going to frown or sulk any more. I won't be ugly. I won't be cross. I won't grow up into that ugly, miserable old man I saw in the magic mirror!"

So he stopped frowning and smiled instead. He laughed instead of grumbling. He was friendly, and soon he had plenty of friends.

Did you know that we make our own faces? We can be just what we want to be, so go and look in the mirror once or twice, and make up your mind what face you want to grow – a kind and smiling one, or a cross and frowning one. You can choose for yourself.

The Boy with a Thousand Wishes

There was once a sharp boy called Gordon. He longed and longed to meet a brownie or a pixie, or someone belonging to the little folk, because he wanted to ask for a wish.

"Just one wish," said Gordon to himself. "Only just one! Surely they wouldn't mind me having just one."

Well, his chance came one morning when he was walking so quietly that a brownie who was sitting under a bush, half asleep, didn't see him until Gordon was right on top of him. The brownie tried to scramble away into the bush – but Gordon put out a long arm and caught him.

"A brownie at last!" said Gordon, pleased. "Good! No – it's no use struggling – you can't get away!"

The brownie stopped struggling at once. He was a tiny fellow, only just as high as Gordon's knee, and his eyes were as green as moss in the sunlight. His beard almost reached the ground.

"Let me go," begged the brownie.

"What will you give me if I do?" asked Gordon, keeping a tight hold of the little fellow.

"What do you want?" asked the green-eyed brownie sulkily.

"I want a wish," said Gordon firmly.

"A wish! Just one wish?" said the brownie in surprise. "Most people ask for three."

"One wish will do very well for me," said Gordon. The brownie stood straight up and looked closely into Gordon's eyes.

"Take my advice and do not ask for a wish," he said. "You'll be sorry!"

"I want a wish," said Gordon. He shook the little fellow hard. "Now, hurry up, or I'll take you home with me."

"You can have your wish," said the brownie, and his eyes gleamed like green stones. "Let me go!"

"Not till I've wished my wish!" said Gordon. "And this is what I wish – that I may have a wish granted every hour of the day and night!"

The brownie pulled himself free and began to laugh. "You think you're clever, but you're not!" he called in his high little voice. "Have all your wishes – but you'll be sorry!"

17

He disappeared behind a tree. Gordon rubbed his hands in glee. He felt quite sure that he would never be sorry.

"I wonder nobody has ever thought of this before!" he said to himself as he went home. "One magic wish can bring as many other wishes as I like! Why people ask for three and then just use them for three silly things and no more puzzles me! Now I can have a wish granted every single hour!"

It was a long way home, and Gordon felt tired. He stood still and thought. "I don't see why I shouldn't have my first wish now!" he said. "Well – I wish for a fine motor-car to take me home!"

There was a bang – and out of the air appeared a red motor-car! At the wheel sat a fat gnome with a most unpleasant face. He grinned at Gordon.

"Good morning!" he said. "I'm your wish-gnome. I have to grant you a wish every single hour. The very first time you forget I'll take you off with me, and you shall be my slave! Then you will have to do my wishes!"

"You be careful, or I'll wish you away!" said Gordon sharply.

"Well, if you do that, your wishes won't come true any more, because I'm the fellow that grants them!" said the gnome. "Now hop in and I'll take you home!"

Gordon hopped in. He thought it was a pity that he had to have a wish-gnome to grant his wishes. When he got home his mother and father, brothers and sisters were most astonished to hear his story and see his fine new car.

"Wish me a silk frock!" cried Elaine.

"Wish me a car like yours!" cried John.

"Wish me, wish me, wish me . . ." shouted everyone.

"I'll wish what I like," said Gordon. "Be quiet, everyone! I shall have twenty-four wishes each day and night, and I will wish us riches, a castle, servants and anything else we want. This gnome is my wish-gnome and he has to grant all my wishes!"

Well, all that day, each hour that came, Gordon wished. He wished for a castle. *Bang!* It appeared on the hill nearby!

The whole family went to see it and chose their own rooms.

He wished for servants. *Bang!* They all appeared, one after the other, bowing low. He wished for money to buy fine food. *Bang!* A great purse of gold appeared in his hand, and Gordon sent the servants out to buy meat, fish, eggs, cakes, biscuits – everything he could think of! What a feast they all had!

By the time it was eight o'clock, Gordon had the castle, servants, gold, fine suits and dresses for everyone, a car for each of them, a throne of gold, and a bed of silver. He had never felt so grand in all his life.

He was very tired with all the excitement. "I'm going to bed," he said to the wish-gnome. "Wake me at eight o'clock tomorrow."

"But you have to wish a wish each hour of the night!" said the gnome. "Don't you remember that you wished for a wish to be granted every single hour of the day and night?"

"Good gracious! Surely you don't mean

I've got to wake up every hour and wish!" cried Gordon. "I'll save them all up and wish twelve wishes tomorrow morning."

"Oh no, you won't," said the gnome with a grin. "You'll just keep to what you said. I'll wake you up each hour to wish."

So poor Gordon had to wake up each hour and wish something. He was so sleepy that it was difficult to think of things. He wished for a golden bicycle, a cat with blue eyes, a goldfish in a big bowl, three singing birds, and many other things.

The next day he went on wishing. He wished himself a crown. He wished himself a kingdom. He wished his mother a golden ring with big diamonds in it. He wished his father a pipe rimmed with precious stones.

His brothers and sisters quarrelled about his wishes. They were always wanting him to wish something for them, and they could never wait their turn.

"Oh, do stop quarrelling!" begged Gordon. "I should have thought that being so rich, and having such wonderful

things to wear and to eat, you would have been very happy. Instead, you quarrel and fight, and disturb me all the time."

It was such a nuisance having to wake up each night and wish every hour. "I really can't be bothered to wake up tonight," said Gordon to the wish-gnome one night. "I'll go without my wishes."

"Gordon, if you do that, you'll be in my power and I'll whisk you away!" cried the gnome in delight.

Gordon looked at the gnome. He couldn't bear him. "How can I get rid of you?" he asked. "I really don't feel as if I want anything else now, and it's a great nuisance to have to think of a wish every hour!"

"You can only get rid of me if you ask me to do something I can't do!" said the wish-gnome, grinning. "But as I can grant every wish, it's not likely you'll be able to do that. I shall just stay with you till you get so tired of wishing that you'll stop – and then I shall whisk you away and make you do my wishes."

So poor Gordon went on and on wishing each day and night. He longed to get rid of the gnome. He set him all kinds of impossible things to do – but the gnome did them all!

Gordon wished for seven blue elephants with yellow ears. He was sure there were none in the world! But the gnome brought them all right, and very peculiar they looked, standing in the courtyard, waving their blue trunks about!

24

It didn't matter what the boy wished, his wishes came true. And all the time his family squabbled and fought, each trying to get Gordon's wishes for themselves.

"Wish me a new white horse!" screamed Fanny.

"Wish me three black dogs!" shouted Ken.

"Wish me a more comfortable bed!" cried Elaine.

"You be quiet, Elaine! It's my turn to

have a wish!" said John fiercely, and he pulled Elaine's hair. She slapped his face. He ran after her, and she bumped into Gordon, knocking him down. John trod on him.

Gordon leaped to his feet in a rage. "How dare you! How dare you!" he yelled. "I'm a king! I won't have you treating me like this!"

"Pooh! You're only Gordon, really!" said Elaine rudely.

"Oh, I am, am I?" said Gordon fiercely. "Well, you're only Elaine. I wish all my wishes undone! May everything be as it was before! I'm tired of all this!"

Bang! The castle vanished. The servants disappeared. Their rich clothes became the poor ones of before. The whole family found themselves in their cottage, staring in fear and surprise at one another.

"Serves you right!" said Gordon. "You don't deserve good fortune. You were much nicer when you were poor and hard-working. And so was I!"

He sat with his head in his hand,

26

unhappy and puzzled. To think that he
had all the wishes in the world and yet
was not so happy as when he had none!
It was too bad.

In an hour's time the wish-gnome
appeared, grinning. "Well!" he said. "Do
you want to wish your castle back?"

"No, I don't," said Gordon. He snatched a boiling kettle off the stove. "Freeze this boiling water!" he said. "Go on! I'm hot and I want ice to suck. Freeze this hot water."

Well, the gnome did everything he could to make that water freeze, but of course he couldn't. No one can make hot water into ice – it just won't happen!

The gnome threw down the kettle,

looking angry. "It can't be done!" he said. "It's impossible. Wish something else that I can do, or I shall disappear for ever and you won't be able to have another wish come true all your life long."

"Then disappear!" cried Gordon. "Go! I don't want any more wishes!"

Bang! The gnome went – and that was the last time Gordon ever saw him. No more of his wishes came true – but he didn't care! It was a better thing to live happily in a cottage with his family, and to work hard, and laugh, than to live in a huge castle with nothing to do but quarrel and fight.

"I thought I was so sharp, only asking for one wish in order to have thousands," said Gordon to himself. "But I was stupid! I'll never do it again."

He needn't worry. He won't get the chance!

The Thrush and His Anvil

It was a lovely spring morning. The birds were singing and the sun shone into Jane's room so brightly that she woke up early and jumped out of bed without waiting for her mother to come and call her.

"I must go out and see how my plants are getting on," she thought. "We have had so many wet days lately that I have not been out in the garden for quite a long time. I'll go before breakfast, while it is fine."

She dressed quickly and ran out into the garden. The air smelled warm and moist after the rain.

Jane had a little piece of garden of her own which she looked after with special care, and she hoped to find that her plants had grown quite big. So they had, but, oh dear! nearly every leaf had a piece bitten off it! Jane was most upset. She ran round the rest of the garden, and found that Daddy's plants were just the same. Lots of his young lettuces were eaten too.

She rushed back to the house and burst into the dining-room where her parents and Peter were sitting down to breakfast.

"Daddy," she cried, "something is eating all our young plants! Something

big too – not just a caterpillar or a grub."

"It's probably the snails," said her father. "After all, they have about fourteen thousand teeth on their tongues, you know. They can do a lot of damage in one night! And there are generally a lot of them about after rain."

"Gracious – have snails got teeth on their tongues?" said Peter. "I never knew that. Fourteen thousand teeth – why, their tongues must be like rasps, then!"

"They are," said Father, "like files. Of course, they are not the kind of teeth you and I have, Peter! But they are very strong, and a snail can eat most of a young plant in a night, using his ribbon-tongue."

"But doesn't he wear it out?" asked Jane.

"Yes, but it is always growing," said Father.

"Well, what are we to do about our snails?" asked Jane. "We can't let them eat everything in the garden. There must be dozens of them about."

"Finish your breakfast," said her

father, "and then we will go and look at the damage."

They were soon out in the garden and looking at the plants.

Suddenly Father stopped and pointed to something.

"Look at that!" he said. "We needn't worry much about your plague of snails. Somebody else knows about them and is dealing with them. See that stone?

That is the thrush's anvil – the place he comes to when he has caught a snail and wants to smash its shell."

The children saw a flint beside the path. Round it were scattered many fragments of broken shell.

"Did the thrush really have the sense to come and use this stone for an anvil?" said Peter, half doubtful.

"Well, come into the summerhouse here and we'll watch," said Father. "It's always better to see a thing for yourself than to hear about it second-hand. Come along."

They sat down in the summerhouse and waited. They didn't have to wait long. Soon a thrush with a speckled breast flew down to the stone.

"He's got a snail in his beak!" whispered Jane.

So he had. Then he began to deal with the snail. He struck it hard on the stone anvil again and again. *Tap, tap, tap, tap! Tap, tap, tap, tap!*

"I've often heard that noise before and I didn't know what it was!" whispered

34

Peter. "Now I shall know it's a thrush using his anvil!"

The thrush worked hard. The snail-shell was strong and it wouldn't break. The thrush beat it down with all his might. *Crack!*

"It's broken!" said Jane. "Now he can get at the soft body inside. He's eating the snail, Daddy."

"Poor snail!" said Peter. "But he shouldn't eat our lettuces!"

"Clever thrush!" said their father, getting up. "Well – I think you can leave him to deal with your snails, don't you?"

The Foolish
White Horse

In Farmer Giles's field there were sixteen horses. Some were brown, some were black, and one was white. Because he was the only white one Punch thought himself very grand indeed.

"You others are common horses," he said. "I am white, and I should be your king."

"Don't be silly," said the other horses, and turned their broad backs on him. Punch trotted over to the pond and had a look at himself in the still water.

"My mane is rather long and untidy," he said. "I think it should be cut. Perhaps if I make myself very smart indeed the others will have me for king."

So he waited until the little brownie from over the hill came riding by on his fairy horse the next full-moon night. The fairy horse was white too – as white as snow. Its mane had sparkling diamonds plaited into it and its tail was cut short and clasped with shining rubies. It was a very beautiful horse indeed.

"Ho, brownie!" neighed the big white horse, galloping up to the brownie. "I want you to do something for me!"

"With pleasure!" said the brownie.

"I want my mane cut short; and my tail clipped like your fairy horse's is," said Punch.

"Oh, I shouldn't have that done," said the brownie. "You might be very sorry."

"I want it done," said the white horse sharply. "I mean to be king of all the horses in this field, and if I make myself very smart and beautiful they will not be able to say no to me! Go and fetch your big scissors, brownie, and do what I ask."

"Well, you will repent it," said the brownie, and rode off to get his biggest pair of scissors. When he came back the big white horse stood very still while the brownie clipped his mane.

"I want it shorter still!" Punch cried impatiently. "Make it so short that it stands up straight like a brush! I want to be really smart!"

So the brownie clipped and clipped until all the lovely mane was gone and only a short row of bristles stood up on the horse's neck.

"Now my tail," said the horse, and

turned round so that the brownie could cut it.

"You have such a nice long, swishy tail," said the brownie. "I really shouldn't have it cut, white horse, I am sure you will be sorry."

"Do as you are told!" said Punch, crossly. So the brownie cut his long tail and made it into a short stump. The white horse went and looked at himself in the pond by the light of the moon, and he was very pleased.

"Oh, I do look smart!" he said in delight. "All the other horses will look most untidy beside me!"

The next morning, how surprised the brown and black horses were to see the white horse and his clipped mane and tail! They ran round and round him, and he stood proudly in the middle.

"Am I not grand?" he said, with a proud neigh. "Am I not the finest, smartest horse you ever saw? Will you not make me your king?"

Then all the brown and black horses save one said yes, they would let him be their king. But the one that shook his head was an old, wise horse, and he neighed a loud laugh.

"Oho!" he said. "You may be grand, but it isn't grandeur that makes a good king – no, it's wisdom! And are you wise? No, white horse, you are the most foolish horse I have ever met in my life! Let the others make you their king, if you like, but my king you shall never be!"

"Why do you think I am so foolish?" Punch asked crossly.

"You will see when the summer comes," answered the old horse and trotted off to eat some long grass in the corner of the field.

Now the white horse was very happy indeed. He was followed about by the other horses, and they praised and flattered him, saying how smart he looked, how beautiful his mane was and how splendid his stumpy tail.

"Why cannot we have our manes and tails cut like that?" they said. So when the brownie came again on the next full-moon night they all cantered over to him and begged him to fetch his scissors for them.

But to their great surprise and rage, the old wise horse galloped up to the brownie and forbade him to do anything of the sort. "Very well," said the brownie, cantering off on his fairy horse, glad to be let off the task of clipping and cutting fourteen manes and tails. The other horses were very angry. They tried to kick and bite the old wise horse, but he neighed so angrily that they grew afraid.

"Wait until the summer comes, and then if you still want your manes and tails cut I will let you do what you wish," said the old horse. "You may bite me and kick me then, if you like – but just wait until the summer comes, I beg of you!"

So they waited – and with the hot weather came thousands of flies. They buzzed round the horses, settled on their eyes and noses, bit their velvet sides and legs, and nearly sent the horses mad. How they swished their tails to get rid of

the flies! How they shook their flowing manes and brushed off the tiresome insects with the long, wiry hairs!

All except one horse. He had no mane and no long tail to swish the tormenting flies away! The smart white horse stood in misery, twitching his ears and skin, trying to get rid of the flies that settled on him everywhere.

Then he began to see how wise the old horse was. How he wished he had a long mane and a tail, no matter how untidy and straggling they were! He was so miserable all day that he didn't know what to do with himself at all.

"Pooh!" cried the other horses, seeing him unable to rid himself of the buzzing flies. "Pooh! A fine king you are, having your mane and tail clipped, and wanting us to have ours done too! Why, we would be in dreadful misery if we had our manes and tails as short as yours! You are not fit to be a king. We will make the old wise horse our king, because he was clever enough to know what was good for us and what was not!"

So they made the old horse their king, and he was as pleased as could be, although he pretended it made no difference to him at all!

He had a kind heart as well as a wise head. When he saw Punch, the white horse, standing miserable and alone, tormented by the flies that he could not get rid of, he bade the other horses surround him. Then, as their tails swished here and there, they flicked the flies from Punch as well as from themselves, and he was very grateful.

The sixteen horses are still there in Farmer Giles's field but you will not see any short-tailed, short-maned horse there now! No, the white horse has grown sensible, and let his mane and tail grow as quickly as they could. He has learned his lesson, you see.

Happy
New Year!

It was the very last day of the Old Year, and the very last hour of it, too. The village clock had just struck eleven. Only one more hour to go until the first day of the New Year!

In the little village of Tippy-Top people were having parties. Tweaky the pixie had six friends to supper. Jimmy the goblin had five. Dame Patty-Pan had seven. Old Man Barley had goodness knows how many.

They were having a very merry time. "And as soon as midnight comes, and the Old Year has gone, we will all go out together and shout 'Happy New Year' through the letterbox of every house," said Old Man Barley. "And what is more, we will take out drums and whistles to welcome the New Year in!"

Everyone was pleased to think of making such a noise. "Nobody will be asleep, because everyone is having a party or sitting up late," said Dame Patty-Pan to her friends. "They will like having 'Happy New Year' shouted through their letterboxes."

Now Snoopy, the imp, knew quite well that many people would be at parties that night and would leave their cottages empty. He knew that Mother Clever-One would leave her house empty, too, to go to Dame Patty-Pan's party.

"And she's got more good spells and bottles of magic than anyone else in the world," thought Snoopy. "I'll sneak in through her window and snoop round to see what I can find. I'll be rich if I can slip away with some of her spells. My, she's got some beauties!"

So that night he crept out into the dark. He passed lighted windows and saw people having fun at parties. Snoopy hadn't been asked to any party at all. Nobody had wanted to invite him.

He came at last to Mother Clever-One's house. He slid quietly through the gate. He came to the window. Ah! It was open. Good! He slipped in at the window and found himself in a dark room.

He drew the curtains behind him and lit a candle. Mother Clever-One's black cat sat and blinked at him. "Just say one

48

single mew and I'll fill the bath and make you swim in it!" said Snoopy, fiercely. So the cat said nothing at all.

Snoopy began to hunt round. Ah! A bottle of invisible paint, a box of yellow growing powder and a tin of good dream spells! Lovely! He set them all on a table together.

And then the village clock struck twelve. At once everyone's doors were flung open and out came the villagers. They ran down the street, calling "A Happy New Year! Happy New Year!" through all the letterboxes.

Somebody came to Mother Clever-One's house and yelled through the letterbox at the top of his voice:

"HAPPY NEW YEAR!"

Snoopy almost jumped out of his skin. He dropped the bottle he was holding. Before he could pick it up someone else came to the letterbox and yelled through it again:

"HAPPY NEW YEAR!"

Snoopy didn't know they were shouting that. He thought they were shouting "FANCY YOU HERE! FANCY YOU HERE!"

"How do they know I'm here?" he thought in fright. "Oh, dear – is it because I've got the candle alight?"

"HAPPY NEW YEAR!"

That was someone else shouting through the letterbox. Snoopy blew out the candle in alarm. "They shouted 'Fancy you here' again," he said to himself. "Oh, dear – they *must* know I'm here then – what will they do to me?"

Well, the next thing he heard was the tremendous noise made by the beating of the drums and the blowing of the whistles to give the Old Year a send-off and the New Year a welcome. *Bang-diddy-bang! Boom-boom-boom! Tee-tee-*

51

tiddley-tee! Boom-boom-BOOM!

"Off you go, off you go!" shouted the villagers to the Old Year, and then banged again to welcome in the New.

Snoopy heard "Off you go, off you go!" and he felt certain they were shouting this at him. He was terrified at all the noise, too. Was a whole army of villagers marching against him?

He ran to the back door. He undid it with trembling fingers. The big black cat watched him. What was the matter with this nasty little creature now? Out went Snoopy into the night, fell into Mother Clever-One's duck-pond, waded out dripping wet, caught his clothes on the wire at the bottom of the garden, rolled down into the ditch there, and then fled for his life over the fields.

"Happy New Year! Happy New Year!" he heard as he went, and again he thought it was "Fancy you here! Fancy you here!" But it was his own guilty mind that made him think that! Silly Snoopy to be so scared of good wishes! It served him right.

Nobody could imagine where or why Snoopy had gone when they found his cottage empty the next day. "Well – it's good riddance to bad rubbish, that's all I can say," said Mother Clever-One. "He never was any good, that's certain!"

He never will be, either – and when the next New Year comes, what a shock he'll get again. Happy New Year! What will he think it is next time?

The
Secret Garden

"We're all going to catch the bus and go into the country on Saturday morning," said Janey, looking round at the other children. "And do you know why? It's to pick primroses and get pussy-willow to take to Miss Brown."

"Oh, that is a good idea!" said Lucy. "She's been ill for a whole week now, and nobody has been able to take her any flowers because they are so dreadfully dear. I looked at some daffodils in the flower shop yesterday – and they were so expensive! I didn't have enough money!"

Miss Brown was the children's teacher. She was very kind to them and they liked her very much. They had missed her that week while she had been at home ill. It would be fun to go with the big girl, Janey, and get primroses and pussy-willow to take to her. They made plans to meet, and Janey told them they must be sure to catch the ten o'clock bus.

"Meet at the park gates," she said. "That's just near the bus stop. Bring your baskets."

Lucy ran home and told her mother. "Well, that is a nice idea," said Mother. "Janey's always kind – but then she has a kind mother. Kind mothers make kind children!"

On Saturday morning Lucy was at the park gates much too early with her little basket. She looked for the others. There was no sign of Tom, Peter, Hannah, Mary, Carol or Janey. She must be very, very early!

She saw the old park-keeper and asked him the time. "Half-past nine," he said. "Where are you going to with your little basket?"

Lucy told him. "We shall pick lots of primroses and take them to Miss Brown," she said, "so that she will have

56

big bowls of them in her bedroom. They are her favourite flower. And we're going to try and find some pussy-willow, too, because she's very fond of that."

"Yes, that's pretty stuff," said the old man. "See you cut the twigs off neatly, though – don't you go and break the boughs and spoil the bush like some people do."

"Janey's taking a knife," said Lucy.

"She's going to be the only one to cut the pussy-willow. She doesn't like spoiling trees either."

She ran off into the park. If she had half an hour to wait for the bus she would go and look at the white ducks on the pond. She had no bread for them that morning, but perhaps someone else would be there feeding them.

She saw a small boy there, and he threw something into the pond. She ran up, thinking he was throwing bread.

But he wasn't! He was throwing stones. One hit the water with a splash and frightened the ducks so that they scuttled away in fright, quacking loudly.

The boy picked up another stone and threw it at the nearest duck. He just missed it.

Lucy could hardly believe her eyes! Throwing stones at those white ducks? The boy must be mad. She ran up to him at once.

"You're not to throw stones!" she said. "It's cruel. You might hit one of those ducks."

"That's what I'm trying to do," said
the boy, looking all round to make sure
there was no one near except this
interfering little girl. "Silly creatures,
ducks! See me hit that one over there!"

And he threw another stone! It didn't
hit the duck, but it gave it such a scare

59

that it half-swam, half-flew to the other
end of the pond.

Lucy caught his arm. "I shall tell the
park-keeper about you. I shall!"

"Tell-tale!" said the boy at once. "Just
like a girl. Running off to tell tales. Silly
creatures, girls."

"It's not telling tales. I'm only trying to
stop the ducks being hurt," cried Lucy.

"All right – go and tell then!" said the
boy, and threw an extra big stone into
the water.

This time he did hit a duck. It gave a
loud squawk and swam round and round
in a very peculiar manner. The stone had
hit its leg.

"You wicked boy!" cried Lucy, and she
looked so very upset that the boy,

frightened now, ran off at top speed. He disappeared out of the park gates.

Lucy wanted to chase him, but the poor duck was making such a noise that she couldn't bear to leave it. She looked round. There was nobody near at all. What could she do? If only the park-keeper was about now! Then she saw that the other ducks, upset and angry because of the loud squawking of the hurt duck, were pecking the poor thing hard. Oh, dear – this was worse than ever!

Lucy suddenly went down the bank to the edge of the pond. The water wasn't very deep. She took off her shoes and socks and waded in. She reached the squawking duck and the others swam away at once. Lucy picked up the duck and waded out again.

The duck was dripping wet and frightened. It tried to struggle away, but Lucy tucked it under her arm and held it firmly. She was careful not to touch the hurt leg, which hung down as if it was broken.

She climbed back up the bank, and then she saw the park-keeper hurrying towards her.

"What are you doing with that duck?" he shouted. "You naughty girl!"

"It's hurt. A boy threw a stone at it and hurt its leg," called back Lucy. "Oh, please can you help it?"

The park-keeper took the quacking duck and looked at its leg. "Poor thing," he said. "That was that bad boy Bill Potter again, I expect. Just wait till I catch him throwing stones again! You come along with me to my little house, and hold the duck while I put a splint on its leg. Maybe it will mend."

So Lucy went with him to his little house at the back of the park, and there she held the duck while he gently straightened its leg and tied a splint of wood to it.

A clock on the mantelpiece suddenly struck loudly. Lucy gazed at it in dismay. Ten o'clock! Oh dear – the bus went at ten.

She ran to the window – and there was

the bus, rumbling away from the bus
stop on its way to the country and
primroses and pussy-willow. And Lucy
was left behind.

"Oh – the bus has gone," she said.
"And now I can't get primroses with the
others! Oh, dear!"

"Now don't you worry," said the old
park-keeper, tucking the duck under his
arm. "I can take you to where you can
pick primroses all morning long, if you
want to – yes, and little wild daffodils,

too, and maybe a few violets if you want them. And you can cut some furry pussy-willow to put with them."

Lucy gazed at him in wonder. "But where?" she asked. "It's all town round here, except for the park – and there are no flowers we may pick in the park except daisies and dandelions."

"There's a secret garden in this park," said the old man. "And it belongs to me! I made it. I planted everything there. And I built a high wall round it so that naughty boys could not come and pick my flowers or spoil my trees. I will show it to you."

Lucy was astonished. The old man led her through his little house and out at a garden door – and there was the secret garden, surrounded by a high wall!

"Oh – what a lovely place!" cried Lucy, in delight. And so it was. It wasn't very big, but that old gardener had made it with love and endless care. It was a little wild garden, with willow trees, a small pond, banks of grass and moss, and primroses everywhere!

"See my primroses?" said the old man. "And those little wild daffodils under those trees? See that pussy-willow, as furry as little grey kittens? Ah, it's much further out than any in the woods, because these high walls shelter my secret garden, and make everything early!"

"It's beautiful," said Lucy. "Oh, look – there are wild violets, too – and early celandines. And are those bluebell leaves over there?"

"Yes – there's a blue carpet of them here in the early summer," said the park-keeper proudly. "And later on there are hundreds of foxgloves, all dreaming together under those trees. It's all very secret – nobody much knows about it, except those I can trust. I let them come and share it with me."

"What made you think of it?" asked Lucy, stepping out into the warm sunshine of the strange little garden.

"I lived in the country when I was a boy," said the old man. "And I loved the woods nearby. There was a little secret place I liked to go to – and when I came here to this big town and got a park-keeper's job, with a little house and a bit of ground, I thought I'd try and make a little place like the one I loved – all wild and secret."

"It's the best secret I ever saw," said Lucy. "Oh – you're putting the hurt duck

on your little pond! How lovely! Now his leg will get better and none of the other ducks will peck him."

The duck seemed very pleased. It bobbed on the little pond and looked very much at home. "Now," said the old man, "you can fill your basket with the biggest primroses you can find, and some violets too, and a few of the wild daffodils – and you can cut some twigs of that pussy-willow over here. Here's my knife. I can trust you not to spoil the bush."

"But – won't it spoil your lovely little

garden if I pick the flowers?" said Lucy, looking round at the primroses and daffodils.

"Oh, no – there are hundreds of primroses," said the park-keeper. "And it's a pleasure to bring a kind little girl like you here, and let her pick flowers to take to someone in bed. You enjoy yourself for a while. I must go back to the park."

Well, Lucy had never enjoyed herself so much in her life! There she was, quite alone in the secret little garden, told to

pick all the flowers she wanted. A robin came to watch her. A thrush flew in and sat on a branch and sang.

"Mind how you do it!" he sang. "Mind how you do it!"

"Oh, I will," said Lucy, and was careful not to pick too many primroses from one plant, nor to hurt the pussy-willow bush when she cut some furry twigs. Soon her little basket was full.

The park-keeper came back in about an hour, and Lucy showed him her flowers. "I hope I haven't picked too many," she said. "Would you mind if I gave my mother a few? I meant to bring her back some from the country if I had gone with the others this morning."

"Yes, of course, give her some," said the park-keeper. "And now you must go. But first you must promise me something – two things."

"Of course I will," said Lucy.

"Promise me you will only tell your mother about my secret garden, and nobody else!" said the old man.

"I promise," said Lucy.

"And promise me you will come and visit me and see how the duck is getting on," said the park-keeper with a twinkle in his eye.

"Oh, I do," said Lucy, in delight. "Oh, will you really let me into this garden again? Oh, Mr Park-keeper, I am so glad I missed this morning's bus!"

Well, wasn't it an exciting thing to share a secret like that? Lucy skipped home with her flowers and just outside the park she saw the naughty boy who had thrown stones at the duck. He was sitting on a seat, looking very sorry for himself. Lucy suddenly saw that his leg was bleeding, and he had a dirty handkerchief round his knee.

"Oh! You've hurt your leg!" said Lucy, stopping. "And the duck's leg was hurt, too. It was broken!"

"I fell down when I ran away," said the boy. "My leg hurts so much I can't walk on it yet."

"Well!" said Lucy, "I think it serves you right. I was sorry for the duck – but I just can't feel sorry for you. It's a very,

very good punishment for you. I'll help
you home, if you like – but only if you
promise you won't throw stones again."

"I'm not going home yet," said the boy
sulkily, so Lucy left him. How surprised
her mother was when she got home so
early with a basketful of such lovely
flowers!

Lucy told her the secret, and she
listened in delight. "Well, what a lovely
thing!" she said. "And how pleased Miss

Brown will be when she sees such beautiful big primroses, and dear little daffodils and this pussy-willow. You have had a surprising morning, Lucy!"

And now each day on her way to school, Lucy calls at the park-keeper's cottage and has a peep at the duck on the pond, and the little secret garden. The duck's leg is almost better – the primroses are finer than ever – and the bluebells will soon be out!

I wish I could tell you where the little garden is, but it is a secret, so I can't. Wouldn't you love to see it?

One Rainy Night

One dark night two fairies set out to go to a party. They had on new frocks, made of buttercup petals, so the two little creatures shone as bright as gold as they ran through the night.

But they hadn't gone very far before it began to rain. They looked at one another in dismay.

"Our new frocks will be spoilt!" said Linnie.

"We shall be soaked through and tomorrow we shall sneeze and have a cold," said Denny. They crouched under a bush and waited for it to stop. But the rain went on and on.

Presently the two fairies heard voices, and they listened. "It's Flora's toys playing," said Linnie. "That means that everyone has gone to bed. Let's fly in at the window and see if they can lend us a towel to dry ourselves."

So they flew in through the open window. The toys were very pleased to see them.

"I say! Aren't you wet!" cried the teddy bear. "Is it raining?"

"Of course!" said Linnie. "Did you think we had been bathing in a puddle or something?" The toys laughed. The clown went to get a towel out of the doll's-house bathroom. Soon the two fairies were rubbing themselves dry.

"Where are you going to, all dressed up in buttercup gold?" asked the curly-haired doll.

"To a party!" said Linnie. "But it's a long way away – and we shall get wet through as soon as we fly out of the window again. It really is a nuisance. I suppose, Dolly, you haven't two old coats you could lend us?"

The curly-haired doll got excited. "I tell you what I and the straight-haired doll have got!" she said. "We have each

74

got mackintoshes and sou'-westers! Flora had them in her stocking for Christmas, and we wore them when we went out in the rain. They would just fit you two!"

"Oh, do lend them to us!" begged Linnie.

So the curly-haired doll went to get them. But they were hanging up high on a peg, and none of the toys could reach them. The two fairies flew up and got them. Then they put them on, and they really did look nice in them! One mackintosh was red and the other was blue.

"I suppose it's all right borrowing them without telling Flora?" said the teddy bear. "You know, I heard someone say the other day that nobody should ever borrow anything without asking first. And we haven't asked Flora."

"Well – let's go and ask her then," said Linnie. The toys stared at her in surprise.

"We can't do that!" said the bear. "Why, Flora would be awfully surprised if we woke her up and spoke to her in the middle of the night!"

"But wouldn't she think it was a nice surprise?" said Denny. The toys looked at one another. The clown nodded his head.

"Yes," he said, "I believe she would. She is always saying that she wishes we were alive. Well – shall I go and ask her or will you, Denny and Linnie?"

"You toys had better go," said Linnie, so all the toys went trotting across the landing to Flora's bedroom. She was fast asleep in her bed, and the bear wondered how to wake her up. He found her hand outside the sheet and patted it. She didn't wake. Then the clown tugged at the

sheet, and that did wake her!

She sat up and switched on her light. She stared in astonishment at the toys. "I must be dreaming!" she said. "Look at all my toys standing by my bed!"

"No. You're not dreaming," said the bear. "We woke you up to ask you something important, Flora. There are two fairies who want to borrow the new mackintoshes and sou'-westers belonging to the dolls. It's such a rainy night and they are on their way to a party. We didn't like to lend them anything without asking first."

"Quite right," said Flora, getting out of bed. "I really must see these fairies! Where are they?"

"In the playroom," said the bear, and they all went back with Flora. She gazed in delight at the two fairies in their golden frocks and mackintoshes.

"What lovely things you are!" she said. "Oh dear – I wonder if this is all a dream! To see my toys alive and to see fairies, all in one night, is just too good to be true!"

"Thank you for saying we may borrow these things," said Linnie. "We'll go now – and we'll hang them safely on the pegs when we come back!"

They flew out of the window, looking really sweet in the mackintoshes and

sou'-westers. The toys waved goodbye.
Flora went back to bed and fell asleep
again.

At cockcrow Linnie and Denny came
back, after a perfectly lovely party. It was
not raining now, so they could go home
safely. They flew in at the window and
hung the mackintoshes and sou'-westers
on the pegs. The toys were all back in

the toy cupboard and did not stir.

"I wish we could say thank you to Flora," said Linnie. "I wonder how we could."

"I know!" cried Denny, seeing a box of letters in the cupboard. "Look – there are lots of letters in that box! Let's spell the words 'Thank you' in letters on the table. Then Flora will see them in the morning and know we have thanked her for her kindness!"

So they spelled the words "Thank you"

in letters on the table and then flew out of the window. And in the morning, when Flora came into the room, she found the words there and she stared in surprise.

"Look, Mummy!" she said. "Isn't that funny? 'Thank you.' Who put it there, and why, I wonder?"

Then she went red in delight and cried out joyfully, "Oh, I know! Of course! It was the two fairies who said thank you! Oh, Mummy, I thought last night that I dreamed my toys came to wake me up to ask me to lend two dear little fairies my dolls' mackintoshes – but it wasn't a dream after all! Dreams can't say thank you, can they!"

"I shouldn't think so," said Flora's mother. "Well, well – fancy you talking to toys and fairies in the middle of the night, Flora! Whatever will you do next!"

The Lost
Doll's Pram

"Mummy, I do so wish Tibbles wouldn't keep jumping into my doll's pram," said Ellie. "How can I stop her?"

"Well, you could stop her by doing what I used to do, when you were a baby in your pram," said her mother. "You can put a net over the pram so that no cat can jump into it."

"Oh dear – I don't want to do that," said Ellie. "It would be an awful bother to have to do that every time I put my dolls to sleep. I shall shout at Tibbles next time I find her in my doll's pram!"

Ellie found her there the very next morning, curled up under the eiderdown, fast asleep. Didn't Ellie shout! Tibbles gave a miaow of surprise, and leaped out at once. She was never shouted at by

Ellie and she didn't like it at all.

"You are *not* to get into the pram," said Ellie to Tibbles. "I have told you ever so often. You are a naughty little cat. Do you want to smother Rosebud or Josephine by lying on top of them? Shoo! Go away!"

Tibbles ran away – but will you believe it, as soon as Ellie went indoors again, Tibbles jumped right into the pram once more!

She did love that pram. It was so soft inside and so cosy. She loved cuddling down, curling herself up and going to sleep in peace and quiet there.

"It just fits me nicely," she thought. "I can share it with the dolls. They never seem to mind. They don't even kick me."

Now the next day three naughty boys came along with a naughty little girl. They saw some apples hanging on the trees in Ellie's garden, and they crept in at the gate to take some.

Ellie saw them from the window. She rushed out into the garden. "You bad children! That's stealing! Go away and leave my daddy's apples alone."

"Give us some!" shouted the biggest boy.

"No, certainly not. If you had come to ask my daddy properly, he would have given you a basketful," cried Ellie. "But people who steal don't get any. Go away!"

"You're a horrid little girl!" shouted the boy. "We'll pay you back!"

And then Ellie's mother came out and the four naughty children ran away. They came peeping over the wall again the day after – but not to take the apples. They meant to pay Ellie back for sending them away.

"Look – there's her doll's pram,"
whispered the little girl. "Let's take it
away into the park and hide it where she
can't find it. That will teach her to shout
at us and send us away. Quick, Billy –
there's no one about – you slip in and
get it."

Billy opened the back gate, ran into
the garden and took hold of the pram
handle. He wheeled the little pram at
top speed out of the gate. *Slam!* The gate
shut and the four children hurried down
the lane to the park.

"She hasn't got any dolls in the pram," said the little girl. "I'd have thrown them into the bushes if she had!"

What a very horrid little girl she was! She had dolls of her own and loved them – and yet she would have done an unkind thing to someone else's dolls! Well, well – some people are strange, aren't they?

The boys stuffed the pram into the middle of a big bush and left it there.

Then they went back to Ellie's garden to see what she said when she came out and found her pram missing.

She soon came out with her two dolls, meaning to take them for a walk, as she always did each morning. But where was her pram? It was nowhere to be seen! Ellie looked everywhere for it and then she saw the four heads of the giggling children, peeping over the wall.

"Have you seen my pram?" she called.

"Yes," they called back.

"Where is it?" shouted Ellie.

"It's hidden in the park where you can't find it!" called the biggest boy. "Ha, ha! You'll never find it again!"

"Mummy, Mummy, come here!" called Ellie, almost in tears. But her mother had just gone next door and she didn't come. So Ellie had to make up her mind herself what she was going to do.

"I must go and look in the park," she thought. "Oh, dear – suppose it rains? My lovely pram will be soaked. Suppose I don't find it? How am I to know where those bad children have put it?"

87

She put her dolls down just inside the house, ran down the garden again, into the lane and was soon in the park. Now where should she look?

She hunted here and she hunted there. She looked in this bush and that, but she couldn't find her pram.

"Oh dear – there are such a lot of bushes and trees!" thought poor Ellie. "I could look all day long and never find my pram. Where can it be?"

It was very well hidden indeed. Someone else was well hidden there too. And that was Tibbles!

Tibbles had been in the pram when the bad children had run off with it, curled up as usual under the eiderdown, fast asleep. When the children had taken the pram, Tibbles had thought it was Ellie taking the dolls for a walk. She hadn't dared to pop her head up, in case Ellie was cross with her. So she just lay there, wondering why the pram went so fast that morning. Then suddenly it was pushed into the bushes, and was still. Tibbles shut her eyes and went to sleep again.

She woke up after a time and stretched herself. Everything seemed very quiet. Tibbles felt hungry and thought she would jump out of the pram and go and find her dinner. She had forgotten that the pram had been taken for a walk – she thought she was still in garden!

She poked her head out from under the covers and looked round. What was this? She was somewhere quite strange! This wasn't her garden. Tibbles sat right up, very frightened.

Where was she? Where was Ellie?

What had happened? And dear me, was this rain beginning to fall?

It was. Big drops pattered down on Tibbles, and she crouched down. She hated the rain. She suddenly felt very lonely and frightened and she gave a loud miaow.

"MIAOW! MEE-OW-EE-OW-EE-OW-EE-OW!"

Nothing happened except that the rain pattered down more loudly. One enormous drop fell *splash*! on to Tibbles' nose, and she miaowed angrily.

The rain made a loud noise on the bracken around, and Tibbles couldn't think what it was. She didn't dare to jump out of the pram.

"MIAOW-OW-OW!" she wailed, at the top of her voice.

Ellie was not very far off, and she heard this last MIAOW. She stopped. That sounded like a cat's voice! Was there a cat lost in the park, caught in the rain that was now pouring down? Poor thing!

"MEEEEEEEEE-OOOW-OOOOW!"

wailed Tibbles, and Ellie hurried towards the sound. "MEEE-OW!"

"It seems to come from that bush over there," thought the little girl, and went to it. Another loud wail came from the spot.

"Meee-ow-ow-ow! MEE-ow-ow-OW!"

And then Ellie suddenly saw the handle of her pram sticking out of the bush. How delighted she was! She ran to it and gave the handle a tug – out came her doll's pram – and there, sitting in the middle of it, scared and lonely, was Tibbles!

"Oh, Tibbles! It was you I heard miaowing!" cried Ellie, in surprise. "You must have been asleep in the pram again when those children ran off with it. Oh, Tibbles, I am glad you were in it – it was your miaowing that made me find it! I'll never scold you again for getting into the pram!"

She put up the hood and drew the waterproof cover over Tibbles so that the frightened cat shouldn't get soaked. And then off she went home with her precious pram, not minding the rain in the least because she was so pleased to have found her pram again.

Tibbles couldn't imagine why Ellie made such a fuss of her, but she liked it all the same. The funny thing was that she never, never got into the doll's pram again. She was so afraid it would run off with her into the park and lose her!

So do you know what she does? She gets into the doll's cot up in the playroom and goes to sleep there! I've seen her, and she really does look sweet, curled up with her tail round her nose.

Clever
Mr Trusty

Mr Trusty was the jolliest, kindest old fellow you could meet. Everyone liked old Mr Trusty, and they went to buy their sweets at his shop each week.

For Mr Trusty kept a sweet and chocolate shop, a lovely place where toffees, peppermints, barley-sugar, pear-drops, chocolates and, in the summer, ice creams were sold.

Mr Trusty gave good value at his shop. People knew they would get their money's worth there. He might even pop an extra sweet or two in the bag if he liked you.

He made all his sweets himself. He was very clever at it. He liked it too – it was fun to see the toffee making itself in the pan, it was fun to twist the barley-sugar and make it pretty, and it was fun to put chocolate round toffee middles.

Mr Trusty sold more and more sweets. What a lot he sold. His shop was always full of people, so that it was sometimes quite difficult for him to slip off to his kitchen and make fresh sweets.

"I'll have to have someone to help me in the shop," he said. "I really shall. But who shall I have? It must be someone I can really trust, because they might keep popping a sweet or two in their mouths when I was not there."

He thought he would get a boy or girl to help him, one who was just leaving school. Yes, that would be a good idea. So he put a notice in his shop window:

WANTED. AN HONEST BOY OR GIRL
TO HELP IN MY SWEET SHOP.
APPLY AT SIX O'CLOCK TONIGHT.

Well, the notice was seen by all the boys and girls, and they were excited about it. To sell sweets! What fun! And old Mr Trusty was so jolly and kind. It

94

would be nice to work for him.

"I shall go and ask for the job," said Sam.

"So shall I," said Jane.

"And I shall too," said Mary. Thomas said the same and so did Greg. They all thought it would be fun to sell sweets – to weigh them out and to put them into a paper bag.

"I could pop one into my mouth sometimes," said Sam to himself. "No one would know."

"I could take a few home in my pocket," said Jane to herself. "Mr Trusty wouldn't know."

But Mr Trusty was going to find out which of the children were honest and which were not. Oh, Mr Trusty might be very kind and very generous, but he wasn't foolish.

The five children went to his little shop at six o'clock. He said he would see them one after another.

Sam went in first. Mr Trusty asked him how old he was and what sort of a school report he had. Then he said, "Oh, excuse me a moment, Sam. I must just go and see to something."

He went out of the room and shut the door. Then Sam saw something gleaming on the floor. It was a nice bright fifty pence piece. Sam stared at it.

He could buy a bar of chocolate with fifty pence. Mr Trusty must have dropped it. Well, what was fifty pence to

Mr Trusty? Nothing much. But it meant a lot to Sam.

Sam stooped quickly and picked it up. He put it into his pocket. After a while Mr Trusty opened the door and came in. "Sorry to keep you waiting," he said. "I see there are other children out there. I'll see them first before I decide. Wait in the garden, will you?"

Jane came in next, and she was asked the same questions. Then Mr Trusty popped out of the room again, and shut the door. And Jane suddenly saw fifty pence shining on the floor!

"I oughtn't to take it," she thought. "I ought to leave it there. But Mr Trusty doesn't know he's dropped it. I could buy some sweets with it."

She bent down and picked it up. Mr Trusty came in again, and then sent for Thomas. The same thing happened – Thomas picked up the fifty pence and put it into his pocket when Mr Trusty went out of the room.

Then in came Greg, and was asked the same questions. Mr Trusty popped out of the room and Greg saw the fifty pence. He picked it up and put it into his pocket. Then he was afraid, because he knew that was stealing, so he put it back on the floor again. But oh dear, he picked it up once more and put it into his pocket just before Mr Trusty came back.

"Well, well," said Mr Trusty, suddenly looking rather sad, "there's only one more child to see. Somehow I don't think I'm going to be able to choose anyone to help me." He called loudly to Mary. "Come along – your turn now."

He asked Mary the same questions

and once more slipped out of the room. Mary saw fifty pence on the floor. She picked it up and held it in her hand.

Mr Trusty came back, and sighed when he saw the coin gone again. Were all children dishonest now?

"Mr Trusty, I saw this coin on the floor," said Mary, and gave it to him. "You must have dropped it out of your pocket."

"Oh, thank you!" said Mr Trusty, joyfully. "How nice to meet a really honest little girl! Will you come and help me in my sweet shop? I can teach you how to make sweets and chocolates, and one day you will be able to have a shop of your own."

"Do you really think I will do the work all right?" said Mary shyly.

"Of course – but the main thing is I shall be able to trust you," said Mr Trusty. "It's dreadful to have people round you that you can't trust, you know. Come tomorrow, will you?"

Mary ran out to tell the others. She told them about the fifty pence she had given back. The other four children remembered the coins they had put into their pockets. They went very red.

Mr Trusty came out. "I've chosen Mary," he said, and smiled at her. "And I've just one word to say to you others – only honest people deserve to get good jobs. What a pity to lose good work for the sake of fifty pence!"

It was, wasn't it? But Mr Trusty knew people who would steal fifty pence would, when they grew older, steal far more than that. That is, if they didn't make up their minds to stop, before it was too late.

It was clever of Mr Trusty to let his coins tell him who was the right person for the job, wasn't it?

It's Really True!

Once upon a time the chestnut tree complained loudly because its buds didn't like the cold.

"The frost comes at night and nips my big buds with icy fingers!" said the chestnut tree, creaking loudly in the winter wind. "What's the use of growing new leaf-buds if the frost kills them one by one? I shall have no leaves left at all next spring. Little folk, come and do something about it!"

So the elves came, tiny creatures who looked after flowers and leaves, who polished the shining petals of the celandines when they blossomed, and rubbed up the little coppery beetles that ran among the grasses in the summer.

"We can wrap your baby leaves in

cottonwool," said the elves. "We'll get some for you."

So they did, and soon every tiny chestnut leaf was wrapped warmly in soft cottonwool; but still the chestnut tree complained loudly.

"The frost still nips my leaf-buds, right through the cottonwool," said the big tree. "I tell you, I shall have no leaves at all. Do something, little folk, or we chestnuts will be bare all summertime!"

So the elves held a meeting, and they made up their minds to paint the big fat buds with sticky glue.

"Nothing like a good coat of glue to keep away the fingers of Jack Frost!" said the elves, and they sat up all night and painted glue over each fat bud.

When Jack Frost came along to pinch the buds with his cold fingers, he didn't like the glue, and he left them alone. So they grew bigger and fatter, and when the right time came they burst out of their glue-coats, grew out of the brown scales that held them, and put out little green fingers which were still wrapped in cottonwool.

Well, any boy and girl knows all this: I should think there is hardly anyone who hasn't picked the fat chestnut buds, felt their stickiness, and put the twigs into water to watch the green fingers unfurl.

Now the plane tree thought all this was a very good idea. It grew next to the chestnut tree, and Jack Frost used to come and pinch the plane tree's buds as well. How they trembled when they felt his cold fingers turning them black and shrivelling them up.

"What am I to do?" said the plane tree. "I have my leaf-buds wrapped up so well. The tiny leaves are wrapped in a quilt of soft silky down to keep them warm. They are covered up well in tiny scales that are covered with soft fur. And the outer case of the bud is lined with sticky gum, as strong as any mackintosh."

"You grow your buds too small," said the chestnut tree. "Grow them fat and big like mine – and when the bitter days of the New Year come, they will be strong."

"It's on the cold days of autumn that

my buds feel the cold so much," said the plane tree. "What else can I do for them? They cannot be more warmly wrapped up than they already are."

"Ask the little folk," said the chestnut tree. "What are they for if not to help us?" So the plane tree called the elves and told them its troubles.

"You must think of some plan to protect my baby leaves in the autumn," said the plane tree. "It is then they feel the cold, and they become so weak that they do not grow well in the New Year. What can I do?"

This was a puzzle. After all, the plane tree already wrapped its leaves in down, and covered them with furry scales. The sticky gum inside their outer case was very strong too. Really there seemed nothing else to do to help the weak baby leaves.

And then an elf had a bright idea. She whispered it to the others. "Can it be done? It's never been done before! It will take us a long, long time – but we'll try it!" they said.

The elves flew that night to the plane tree, which was still covered with its summer leaves. The elves worked very hard indeed, all night long – and what do you think they did?

They took every leaf from its twig.

They hollowed out the leaf-stalk at the bottom, making it round and large and empty. And then, instead of fitting back each leaf in the place it grew, they carefully fitted the end of the hollowed out stalk over the little new leaf-buds that were already showing on the twigs!

"The leaf-stalks fit over next year's buds like little caps!" said an elf, pleased. "I say, isn't this a good idea! The little buds will be well protected now. Jack Frost can hunt all he likes for the buds on the plane tree, but he won't find them! They're all hidden at the bottom of the stalks of the autumn leaves!"

The elves flew away, tired out with their night's work. Jack Frost came along at night, hunting for tender leaf-buds to nip. He came to the plane tree – and how he stared!

"I can't see a single bud on the tree!" he said. "Not one! Where are the next year's buds? I can see the autumn leaves - but not a bud is to be seen, though there are plenty on the other trees!"

He hunted up and down the plane tree,

but he couldn't find the buds. They were too well hidden under the leaf-stalks, which fitted over them most perfectly.

After that Jack Frost didn't bother to hunt for plane buds any more. They nestled under the bottom of the old leaf-stalks, safe and sound, warm and cosy. And when the leaves fell off there were tiny buds underneath, well-grown and strong, ready to burst into new leaves in next year's spring.

This sounds like a fairy-story, doesn't

109

it? That's what everybody says. And yet – it's a very funny thing, but it's really true that the leaf-stalks are hollowed out to fit over the new-growing little buds on every plane tree! Will you look and see, when the plane tree has grown its big leaves, and is changing colour in the autumn?

Don't forget. You won't see a single bud on the tree – but pull away a leaf and you'll find a new bud nestling underneath. Isn't it a clever idea?

Blue Shoes
for the Party

"Mummy!" cried Ann, dancing into the kitchen, where her mother was making cakes. "I've got an invitation to Lucy's party. May I go?"

"If you're a good girl," said her mother. "You can wear your new blue dress."

"But what about shoes?" asked Ann. "I haven't any blue ones to match, Mummy. And my old party ones are no use now because they don't fit me."

"Well, perhaps I'll buy you a new pair of blue ones," said her mother. "But you must just show me how good you can be, Ann, or I certainly shan't buy you any."

Ann made up her mind to be as good as gold. But somehow or other things seemed to go wrong. Ann dropped one of her mother's very best cups and broke

it. Then she dropped a bowl of flowers she was carrying, and that broke too, and all the water went on the carpet.

Ann's mother was cross.

"You're a careless little girl," she said.

Ann said she was sorry. She did hope her mother wouldn't be cross enough not to buy her the blue shoes. She determined to be very careful indeed for the few days before the party.

Soon another unlucky thing happened. Ann lost her new socks! Then her mother was really cross!

"You'll have just one more chance!" she said to the little girl. "If you do one more careless or naughty thing you shall not have your new shoes!"

Ann knew that her mother meant what she said, and she began to be really afraid she wouldn't be able to go to the party. So for the next two days she was a very good little girl indeed.

Then came the day before the party.

"Mummy, may I go and buy those new blue shoes with you?" asked Ann.

"Yes," said her mother. "I'll take you this afternoon. But this morning I want you to take a message for me to Mrs Robinson. Here is the note. Now go straight there and back. You just have got time before lunch, so don't dawdle as you did last time. If you do, lunch will be cold, and we shall probably miss the only bus into the town to get your shoes."

"All right, Mummy!" said Ann, happily. "I'll be sure to be back in time!"

113

Off she ran with the note. She went down the lane, and over the stile into the fields. Soon she came to the wood, and took the path that ran through it. She didn't stop for anything, not even when she saw some lovely foxgloves blooming all together.

When she arrived at Mrs Robinson's, Ann gave her the note, took the answer, and turned to go home again.

"I shall be home before Mummy expects me!" she thought.

Now, as she went back through the wood, she chanced to hear a cry. It was a funny sort of sound, not like a bird or animal. Ann wondered what it could be. She stopped a moment, and looked through the trees where she thought the cry had come from. And as she stopped someone came running out from the trees towards her.

Ann stared in surprise – for it was an elf! He was very small, tinier than Ann, and he was crying.

"Little girl, little girl," he cried, "come and help me! My butterflies are all entangled in the thorns!"

Ann ran through the trees to where he pointed. There she saw an astonishing sight. There was a beautiful little carriage, drawn by five blue butterflies, but somehow or other they had got themselves caught in a bramble bush, and their pretty wings were being torn as they struggled to free themselves.

"Could you help me?" asked the elf, drying his eyes. "If you could hold the reins tightly I think I could get their wings free. But it will take rather a long time."

"Oh, dear!" said Ann, in dismay. "I'd love to help you, little elf, but my mother says I must get home quickly. You see, she's going to take me into town to buy me a pair of blue shoes for tomorrow's party, and if I'm late she won't take me, and anyhow we should miss the bus. I'm afraid I can't stop to help you."

"All right," said the elf, tears streaming down his face again. "I quite understand. But, oh, my poor butterflies! They'll be torn to bits. If you meet another little girl who hasn't got to buy shoes for the party would you tell her to come and help me?"

Ann looked at him, and then looked at the butterflies. She knew quite well that she wouldn't meet anyone else going through the woods. She didn't know what to do.

Then she suddenly made up her mind.

"Don't cry," she said. "I'll stay and help. Perhaps I'll be in time for lunch after all."

"Oh, thank you a thousand times!" cried the elf, wiping his eyes. "Come on, then. Hold the reins, and I'll go and calm the butterflies."

Ann climbed into the little carriage, and held the reins firmly. The elf ran to his butterflies and began to disentangle their wings from the cruel thorns. One by

one he freed them. It took a long time, for he was so afraid of tearing their beautiful wings. But at last it was done.

"There!" he said, joyfully. "They're all free now. Thank you so much, little girl. I do hope you'll be in time."

"I hope so too," said Ann. "Well, goodbye and I hope you get home safely."

She ran off. She knew it must be very late. She ran faster than she had ever run before. She panted and puffed, and didn't stop once till she reached home and ran up the garden path.

"Well!" said her mother. "What in the world have you been doing to be so late? Lunch is over long ago and the bus is just starting."

"Oh, Mummy!" said Ann, nearly crying. "I really couldn't help it. You see, I met an elf and – "

"Nonsense!" said her mother, crossly. "You've been dawdling again. Well, you can't have your blue shoes, that's all."

"But, Mummy, I can't go to the party unless I have them!" said Ann. "I haven't any others I can wear."

"Well, it's your own fault!" said her mother. "You're a silly little girl. Now go and eat your lunch, and don't let me hear a word more."

Poor Ann! She went and sat down at the table, but she couldn't eat anything. She was so dreadfully disappointed. She saw the bus go off, and a big lump came into her throat. No shoes and no party! She was very sad.

She had to look after the baby all the afternoon, and after tea she had some school-work to do. She went early to bed, for she wanted to go to sleep and forget her disappointment.

Early the next morning she got up to get her mother a cup of tea. She opened the front door of the cottage to bring in the milk – and then she stopped and stared in surprise.

On the doorstep was a box. It was bright yellow, and tied with blue ribbon. A little label hung from it that said: *For the little girl who helped my butterflies.*

Ann picked up the box. She quickly took off the ribbon and opened the lid. And, oh my! What do you think was inside? Why, the prettiest, daintiest pair of blue satin shoes you could possibly imagine, and instead of buckles they had two tiny blue butterflies, just like the big ones she had helped the day before.

Ann cried out with joy. She sat down on the doorstep and tried the shoes on. They fitted her exactly – and didn't they look lovely! They were the prettiest pair she had ever seen in her life, far, far nicer than any she could have bought in a shop.

She ran upstairs to her mother.

"Mummy, Mummy!" she cried. "Look, the elf has brought me some shoes for the party! I expect he knew that I couldn't go and buy any because he made me late!"

Then, of course, her mother had to hear all the story, and she was very glad when she knew what had happened.

"Well, you deserve them," she said to Ann. "I really didn't believe you had met an elf, but I do now, for these shoes are fairy ones, if ever shoes were! You will look lovely in them!"

"Hurrah!" said Ann. "Everything has come right now! I shall enjoy the party!" And she did!

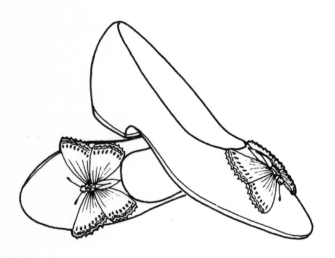

The
Mysterious Thief

Every morning the milkman left a bottle of milk on the doorstep. Billy-Bob used to take it in sometimes, and it felt very cold and slippery. He was careful not to drop it.

"Belinda, look at the cream on the top of the milk," he said each time he brought the bottle in. "We can have it on our porridge!"

It was fun to watch their mother pour the milk into a jug, and then on to their porridge. Billy-Bob and Belinda liked to swish it round their plates. Wags, their dog, liked to lick out the top of the milk bottle if only he could find it somewhere within reach!

One morning, when Billy-Bob went out to get the bottle of milk from the

doorstep, whatever do you think he saw? Why, the milk bottle was upset, the top was off, and the milk was gone!

"Oh, Mum!" cried Billy-Bob, rushing indoors. "Mum! Some one has stolen our milk! Look the bottle is empty. We've no milk for breakfast."

"Oh, what a pity," said his mother, vexed. "Now we shall have to use the little drop I had left over last night. I hope it isn't sour."

"It isn't," said Billy-Bob, when he tasted it. "Mum, who do you suppose stole our milk? Wasn't it a horrid thing to do?"

"A very horrid thing," said Mother. "I can't imagine who it was."

"Perhaps it was that little boy who makes faces at us at the bottom of the road," said Belinda.

"Oh, you mustn't say things like that," said Mother. "He may pull ugly faces, but I am quite sure he wouldn't steal somebody's milk."

"Well, Mummy, who could it be?" said Belinda, stirring her porridge round.

"I don't know," said Mother. "Belinda, don't stir your porridge round any more, you'll make it giddy! Eat it up!"

So Belinda ate her porridge up, and Billy-Bob ate his, and nobody said any more about the stolen milk.

But will you believe it, when Billy-Bob went to get the bottle of milk the next morning the milk was gone again! Yes – it really was! The bottle was once more lying on its side, the top was off, and the milk was gone. There were just a few drops on the step, but that was all.

"Mum, the milk's been stolen again!" yelled Billy-Bob, rushing indoors with the empty bottle.

"Billy-Bob, don't run with a glass bottle," said Mother. "You know that it is a very dangerous thing to do. Oh dear — so the milk is gone again. Well, I haven't a single drop this morning, so you will have to go and ask Mrs White next door if she can lend us some."

Billy-Bob went to ask Mrs White, and she gave him a small jugful because her milk had not been stolen, so she had plenty. Billy-Bob carried it carefully home without spilling a drop. He thought and thought about their own milk, but he simply couldn't imagine who had stolen it.

"Mum, let's put Wags in the hall to sleep tonight," he said. "Then, if any one comes in the early morning after the milkman has left the milk, Wags will hear them and bark. Then they will be frightened and will go away."

"That is a good idea, Billy-Bob," said Mother. "We will put Wags's basket there, and he shall sleep just by the door."

So that night Mother put Wags's basket in the hall by the front door. Wags was surprised. He stood looking up at Mother, wagging his tail as if to say, "All right, Mistress, I will sleep here – but it seems to be a funny thing to do!"

Mother knew what Wags said. She could always read the language his tail

spoke! "It's all right, Wags," she said, patting him. "I just want you to sleep here for a few nights, and then if any bad person comes creeping up the path to steal our milk in the morning you will hear them and bark!"

"Woof!" said Wags, wagging his tail. He jumped into his basket and lay down with his long ears drooping over the edge. He was on guard!

Now the next morning, at about a quarter past seven, Wags heard something. He awoke and sat up in his basket. Some one was scrabbling and scraping on the front doorstep. It was the milk thief! Wags jumped out of his basket and ran to the door. He scraped at it with his feet, barking loudly.

Billy-Bob woke up in a hurry. "Wags is barking at the milk thief!" he cried to Belinda, who had woken up too. "Quick, come to the window and see who it is!"

Billy-Bob and Belinda ran to the window and looked out, but do you know, they couldn't see any one at all! Nobody went down the path in a hurry!

Nobody ran across the garden! It was most mysterious.

"Perhaps it wasn't the robber," said Billy-Bob. But, you know, it was! Because when Father went downstairs and undid the door, there was the milk bottle knocked over again and the milk gone!

"Well, really, this is too bad," said Father. "I shall tell our policeman about it. We can't get up early in the morning and watch over our milk every day. It is silly. The policeman will soon find out who is the thief."

So Father went to see Mr Plod the policeman. He wrote down a great many things in his notebook and looked very serious.

"I haven't heard of anyone else having their milk stolen," he said. "It's very strange, sir, that it's just your milk! I'll keep a watch tomorrow. Do you mind if I hide behind that thick lilac bush in your garden?"

Billy-Bob and Belinda were most excited to think that Mr Plod was going to hide in their garden. They went and looked at the lilac bush and wondered if Mr Plod could really hide there. He was such a big policeman. Billy-Bob got into the bush and pretended to be Mr Plod. It was great fun playing policeman all that day.

Wags didn't sleep in the hall that night. He slept in his usual place in the kitchen. Mr Plod said it would be better not to have him near the door in case he barked too soon and frightened the thief away.

Well, Mr Plod got behind the lilac bush just after the milkman had left the milk.

He couldn't see the front doorstep from
the bush, but he could quite well see if
any one came up the path or crept round
the house. He hid there and waited. He
waited and he waited. Nobody came.
Nobody even went down the street.

When seven o'clock came Mr Plod came out from behind the lilac bush and looked up at Father's bedroom window.

Father opened the window and looked out. "Seen anybody?" he said.

"Not a single person!" said the policeman. "I think the thief must have known I was hiding here this morning."

Billy-Bob ran down to get in the milk for his mother, but dear, dear me, when he opened the front door there was the milk bottle on its side again, and all the milk gone!

Billy-Bob stared as if he couldn't believe his eyes. Really, it was very, very mysterious. How could the milk have been stolen when Mr Plod was hiding behind the lilac bush?

"Mr Plod, Dad, Mum, the milk has been stolen again!" shouted Billy-Bob. And then what a to-do there was! Mr Plod vowed he hadn't been to sleep in the lilac bush, and hadn't seen anyone at all. Wags barked. Billy-Bob told Belinda at the top of his voice all about it.

"Well, sir, I'm very sorry I couldn't see

what happened to the milk," said Mr Plod, looking quite hot and bothered. "I'm afraid I can't hide again tomorrow morning because I'm doing something in the next village. But I'll come again on Friday and try."

"Come and have a hot cup of tea," said Mother. "It must have been cold hiding out there so early in the morning."

So Mr Plod had a hot cup of tea and he said it made him feel better. Then he got on his bicycle and rode away.

"Belinda," said Billy-Bob that afternoon, in an excited voice. "I've an idea. What about me hiding and watching for the thief? If only I can wake up early enough I could actually squeeze into the lilac bush!"

"Oh yes, Billy-Bob, do!" squeaked Belinda. "Let me come too!"

"No, Belinda," said Billy-Bob. "Mum wouldn't like you to do that. You are too little. Besides, it was my idea. I want to do it."

Billy-Bob didn't say a word to his mother about his idea, not a word! He was just a bit afraid she might think he was too little!

"I do hope I wake up early enough in the morning, Belinda," he said, when they were going to bed that night. "Do you think I shall?"

"Oh yes, I expect so," said Belinda. "Just say you want to wake up at seven o'clock, and perhaps you will."

So as he went to sleep that night, Billy-Bob whispered over and over to himself, "I want to wake up at seven o'clock! I

134

want to wake up at seven o'clock!"

And, do you know, when the hall clock was striking seven, Billy-Bob awoke! Wasn't that clever of him? He sat up and listened to the clock striking. And then he heard the milkman coming up the path, he heard the thud of the bottle being put on the doorstep and the milkman going away again. Good!

Billy-Bob dressed very quickly indeed, but he only did up just a few buttons. He put on his coat and crept downstairs. Belinda was fast asleep. Nobody else was

awake either. Billy-Bob had the whole house to himself. He let himself out of the back door. He ran to the lilac bush. He peeped first to see if the milk bottle was on the doorstep, and it was standing up, quite full.

Billy-Bob hid himself in the bush and waited for the mysterious thief. He waited and he waited, just as Mr Plod had done. But he heard no footsteps down the road at all.

Suddenly he heard something else! It was the sound of the milk bottle being tipped over, and yet Billy-Bob had seen no one going up the path to the front door at all! Still, the thief was there. Billy-Bob heard the sound of the milk gushing out! He jumped out of the bush. He ran bravely to the front door, crying "I've got you, I've got you!"

And then he saw the thief! Whoever do you think it was? Guess! It was their hedgehog, the one that Belinda had found at the bottom of the garden!

Would you believe it? He had come every morning to the doorstep, slyly

tipped over the bottle, pushed off the top and then lapped up all the milk that ran out! Oh, you bad hedgehog – whoever would have thought it was you!

Billy-Bob stared and stared. There was the prickly hedgehog, lapping up the milk and making a great noise as he did it! He didn't even stop when Billy-Bob came up to him. He knew Billy-Bob all right; Billy-Bob wouldn't hurt him! Why, he had often had saucers of food from Billy-Bob.

Billy-Bob ran round the house and in at the back door. "Mum! Dad!" he shouted, running up the stairs, "I've found the milk thief! It's our hedgehog! He tipped the bottle over, got off the top, and then drank the milk!"

Well! His mother and father couldn't help laughing. So that was the mysterious thief after all! Just their own naughty hedgehog! Whatever would Mr Plod say when he heard? He would laugh to think he had hidden in the lilac bush to catch a hedgehog!

"You're a clever fellow, Billy-Bob!" said

Father. "You found out the thief when nobody else could! Well done!"

"Daddy, how are we going to stop the hedgehog from stealing our milk each morning?" asked Belinda.

"Oh, ask Billy-Bob that," said her father. "He's very clever; if he can find the thief, he can stop the stealing. What shall we do about it, Billy-Bob?"

"We'll ask the milkman to leave the bottle on the windowsill!" said Billy-Bob at once. Wasn't that a good idea of his? You see, the hedgehog couldn't climb up there!

So now the milk bottle is left on the windowsill, and it is quite safe there each morning. But the hedgehog is not forgotten; he gets a saucer of milk each day. Billy-Bob and Belinda give it to him. He's a lucky fellow, isn't he?

Clever-One
the Imp

At one end of Tick-Tock Village lived the goblin, Gloomy. At the other end lived the witch, Greedy. In between were the cottages of the pixies, elves and imps.

"We're most unlucky," they said to one another when they met at the market each day. "If we don't meet Gloomy, with his bad temper and moans and groans, we bump into Greedy, with her horrid ways. And we don't dare to offend them because they really know more magic than we do!"

Clever-One the imp didn't know Gloomy or Greedy. He had just come to stay with his brother, Poppit, who lived near to Gloomy. He listened to everything that was said, and then he looked very thoughtful.

Poppit looked at him. "He's thinking," he said proudly to everyone. "He's thinking very hard. Soon his head will swell up and we shall know he's got a good idea."

Just then Greedy came by and pushed everyone out of the way. Then Gloomy came up, frowning and muttering, and all the little folk scurried off. But not Clever-One. He still stayed where he was, thinking. His head swelled up and Poppit, who was watching him from a good way off, knew he had suddenly got an idea.

Greedy glared at him and pushed him off the pavement. Gloomy, who was walking in the road, bumped into him, and pushed him back on to the pavement.

"What are you dreaming of?" he growled. "Standing there in everybody's way."

"Dear me, I'm so sorry," said Clever-One, "but the truth is, I was just wondering where in the world I put the magic broomstick that belonged to my grandmother. It would be so useful just now, because my car has broken down. It's a wonderful broomstick, better than any other in the world, because it goes higher and faster."

Gloomy and Greedy stared at Clever-One and suddenly became quite polite to him. "What a wonderful broomstick!" said witch Greedy, who only had a very ordinary one that refused to fly at all on a rainy or a windy night.

"Where can it be?" said goblin Gloomy, who hadn't got a flyaway broomstick at all.

143

"I must find out," said Clever-One. "Yes, I really must. I'll hunt for it till I find it."

"Do let me know when you find it," said Greedy. "I'll buy it from you."

"No. I'll buy it!" said Gloomy, crossly. "She's got one already. Greedy thing!"

"I'll make your nose grow long and then put a knot in it!" said witch Greedy, angrily.

Goodness knows what would have happened if Clever-One hadn't walked off, still looking as if he was thinking very deeply. The goblin and the witch both followed him at once.

They kept him in sight all day and he led them a fine dance. But when night came, and all three were tired, Clever-One made his way to a lonely cave in a hill at the back of the village. Gloomy and Greedy followed him, feeling certain that the imp had remembered the place where his grandmother's broomstick was.

In the cave, sure enough, was a long, strong broomstick, with a fine sweeping-end that had never been used. "Aha!"

144

said Clever-One, loudly. "Here it is." He took hold of it, sat on the stick and galloped round the cave with it.

Greedy and Gloomy both rushed in. They caught hold of the broomstick too.

"Sell it to me!" cried Gloomy.

"No, to me!" shouted Greedy, and they both tried to tug it away.

"Now, now, what manners!" said Clever-One, shocked. "Surely you don't want to break it between you? Now, I'll tell you what I'll do. I'll let you each have a ride on it to see if you like it before you buy it."

"No," said Greedy. "If Gloomy sits on it and rides off, he'll never come back. I know him, the deceitful rogue."

"Ho!" said Gloomy, frowning so hard that his eyes disappeared. "And what about you, madam? I know perfectly well that once you get on it, you'll ride off through the night, and keep the stick for your own for always."

"Dear, dear!" said Clever-One, looking puzzled. "Then I daren't let either of you ride alone. I know! You can take a ride together! That will be a splendid idea."

Greedy and Gloomy looked sharply at Clever-One. "There's a trick in this!" said Gloomy. "I smell it! You're going to send us both off somewhere on this magic broomstick of yours – and you think we'll never come back, so that the village of Tick-Tock will be rid of us!"

"Very well," said Clever-One, looking offended. "If you think that, don't ride the broomstick. I'll have it for myself."

"No. You ride with us!" cried Greedy, and pulled Clever-One down on to the broomstick in front of her. "Get on, Gloomy. Now, if he plays any tricks with us, and sends us off to the moon, he'll go too! Ha, ha, ha!"

"Wait, wait! Let me strap my parcel on my back," said Clever-One as he picked up something from the floor. He put it over his shoulders. "I need both hands to hold the broomstick."

All three sat on the big broomstick, and walked it to the cave entrance. Clever-One suddenly struck the stick hard and cried out loudly. "To the moon! To the moon! And don't come back for a week, old broomstick!"

"You rogue!" cried the witch. "I thought you'd play a trick. But you'll have to come too! Ho, ho! We shall make you our servant up there for a whole week!"

Up into the air went the broomstick with a loud swishing noise like a rocket. The three held on tightly. The broomstick circled round and then went straight up towards the big round moon in the sky.

Was Clever-One frightened? Did he mind what was happening? Not a bit of it!

When they were fairly high up, just reaching the first clouds, Clever-One pulled a cord that hung down in front of him, and was attached to the parcel he carried. Then he suddenly leaped off the broomstick, with such a terrible yell that the witch and the goblin almost fell off in fright themselves.

"He's gone!" said Gloomy. "Good riddance! I hope he lands with a hard bump!"

"He'll think twice before he plays tricks on anyone again," said Greedy. "Nasty little imp! Serves him right."

But Clever-One wasn't about to hurt himself. Oh, no! The parcel he had tied to himself was a neatly folded parachute, and when he pulled the cord, and jumped off into the air, the parachute began to open! Soon it was fully open, and Clever-One began to float gently downwards to earth.

"Here I come!" he shouted to all the folk of Tick-Tock, who had heard the swishing of the broomstick and had come running out to see what was happening. "Here I come! I'm frozen. Somebody get me some hot cocoa!"

"Where are Greedy and Gloomy?" cried Poppit.

"Probably on the moon by now," said Clever-One, coming gently down to earth. "They wanted my broomstick and they got it. We won't see them for at least a week. That will teach them a lesson!"

Tinkle's Party

Tinkle was a pixie, and he lived with his mother in Daffodil Cottage, just at the end of Twiddle Village. He was a merry little fellow, but oh dear me, what a dreadful memory he had!

"Goodness, Tinkle!" his mother said, quite twenty times a day. "Do you remember *anything*? Things seem to go in at one ear and out at the other."

Tinkle did the silliest things. He would make tea for breakfast and forget to put the tea in. He would put salt in his cocoa and sugar on his egg. Once he put his gloves on his feet, and his shoes on his hands; so you can see what a terribly bad memory he had.

Of course he didn't really try to think. He had very good brains and he didn't use them. Then one day he did something that made his mother feel quite upset.

He went to take the dog out for a walk. He saw some fine berries in a field, and he tied the dog to a post while he picked them. He didn't notice that a fine fat cow was tied nearby too. The farmer who owned it had gone into a cottage just near, and left his cow outside for a moment.

When Tinkle had eaten the berries, he went to the post, untied the string, and led off what he thought was his dog – but he had untied the wrong animal and it was the great cow that followed him!

Tinkle didn't notice anything at all. He went on towards his home, and when he got there he took the cow indoors and tried to make it get into his dog's basket.

"Tinkle! Whatever have you brought that great cow indoors for?" shouted his mother in amazement. "Take it out at once! Oh, my goodness, Tinkle, whatever will you do next? You've frightened me

nearly to death! A cow in my nice clean kitchen indeed! I never heard of such a thing in my life!"

"Well!" said Tinkle, looking at the cow in astonishment. "How did that happen now? I quite thought it was the dog. No wonder it couldn't sit down in the basket."

Tinkle's mother felt really quite ill with the fright and very cross too. She talked seriously to Tinkle, and he listened.

"You know, Tinkle," she said, "you are growing into a big pixie now. You will never be any good in the world if you are so forgetful. Now, will you promise me to try and do much better?"

Tinkle's mother looked so solemn and stern that Tinkle was frightened. He began to cry, and tears rolled down his nose.

"Oh, Mother," he said, "I really will be better! I'll never forget anything again! Do forgive me and give me one more chance."

"Now, don't cry," said his mother. "I will give you another chance, and I'm sure you will do better."

Now that afternoon a parcel arrived for Tinkle's mother. In it were three beautiful cakes, lots of small buns, a box of chocolates, a tin of biscuits, and some lovely red apples.

"All this is from your Aunt Tippitty," said Tinkle's mother, pleased. "Isn't she a kind soul? Now, Tinkle, I'll give you a treat. You've been a good pixie today since you promised to think hard, so I'll tell you what I'll do. You shall have a party tomorrow and eat all these good things!"

"Ooh, Mother!" cried Tinkle, in delight. "Thank you very much."

"Sit down and write twelve invitations in your best handwriting," said his mother. "This is what you must say:

"Please can you come to a party

tomorrow at four o'clock? Don't bother to answer, but just come. With love from Tinkle."

So Tinkle sat down and did just what he was told. His mother looked over the notes and saw that they were nicely written.

"Here are the stamps," she said. "Stick them on, and then you can run out and post the letters."

Tinkle stuck on the stamps. Then he put on his hat, put the letters carefully into his pocket, and went out to the post.

He was so excited about the party! It was the first one he had ever had. When he got back home he made out a list of games to play, and set out all his toys neatly, so that his friends might see them when they came.

"Now, you must help me this morning," said his mother next day. "You will want fourteen chairs, so you must get them from the different rooms and set them round the table. Then you must go and buy me some fresh butter. After that you can get out your best clothes and make sure that there are no buttons missing."

How hard Tinkle worked, and how happy he was!

"Mother!" he said, "I've not forgotten a single thing. I'm very clever. I'm sure I shan't forget things any more. I'm quite cured."

At three o'clock Tinkle dressed himself in his best clothes. He set the table, and how his mouth watered to see all the good things! Ooh! what a lovely party it was going to be!

At four o'clock he went to the window to see who would come first. He could see no one in the lane, and he thought that perhaps the clock was fast. Ten minutes went by, and still no one came.

"Well, your guests *are* late!" said his mother, who was busy setting out dishes of jam. "I wonder why. Is there no one in sight yet, Tinkle?"

"No," said Tinkle, looking rather miserable. "Perhaps some of them couldn't come, Mother. Oh, here's someone!"

But it was only the balloon man going to sell balloons at the corner. No one else came down the road for a long time.

The clock struck half-past four.

"Well, this is very strange!" said Tinkle's mother, in surprise. "Whatever has happened to everyone?"

Tinkle was very miserable. There were all the goodies on the table and no one to eat them! His list of games to play was up on the mantelpiece, but there was no one to play them! Why didn't anyone come?

At last, when the clock struck five, and still no one had arrived, Tinkle's mother told him to put on his hat and run to Tick-Tock's to see why he hadn't come. Then he was to go to Flip's and to Gobbo's and ask them too.

So Tinkle ran off. He knocked on Tick-Tock's door, and Tick-Tock's aunt opened it.

"Please," said Tinkle, "why hasn't Tick-Tock come to my party?"

"He didn't know you were having one!" said the aunt in surprise. "He has gone to play with his cousin."

Then Tinkle ran to Flip's and asked Flip's mother why the little pixie had not come to his party.

"What party?" said Flip's mother in surprise. "He didn't know anything about it! He has gone to the zoo."

Well, that was really surprising. That was two people who hadn't heard of the party. And Tinkle got the same reply at Gobbo's.

"Why," said Gobbo's mother, "Gobbo didn't know anything about your party! Did you write to him?"

"Yes," said Tinkle.

"Well, he has gone to see his uncle," said the mother. "I'm very sorry."

Tinkle ran back home, crying. He told his mother all he had done, and she was very much puzzled. "Don't cry, Tinkle," she said. "You're making your eyes so red. Where's your handkerchief?"

"I've left it in my other suit," said Tinkle sniffing. "I'll go and fetch it." He ran to fetch it.

He put his hand into the pocket – and, my goodness, what was this! He pulled out of the pocket twelve letters! Tinkle stared at them in horror. They were the invitations he had written the day before!

"Mother! Mother!" he cried, running into the kitchen with them. "Oh, Mother! I p-p-posted my handkerchief yesterday instead of the l-l-l-l-letters! Oh, boo-hoo-hoo!"

"Well, of all the forgetful sillies!" cried his mother, angrily. "And there's all this good tea wasted! Well, I've no sympathy with you, Tinkle – not a bit. You promised yesterday to use your brains,

and then you go out straightaway and post your handkerchief instead of your party invitations! I shan't bother with you any more. The very next time you do something silly I shall send you to witch Think-Hard, and if she doesn't teach you how to remember, well, nobody will!"

How Tinkle cried! He was so disappointed, and so angry with himself for being so silly. He had punished himself and no one else.

His mother popped a shawl round her shoulders and ran out. Soon she was back again with some of her own friends and they all sat down to enjoy Tinkle's party cakes and buns. No one took any notice of the pixie at all. They all thought he was too silly for anything, to forget to post the invitations for his own party.

Tinkle crept off to bed. He was very unhappy. He knew quite well that his mother really would send him to witch Think-Hard next time.

"Well, I must use my brains now!" he sighed. "I really must! What a silly I am! What a goose, what a cuckoo I am! But in future I will be better!"

And I'm sure you will be glad to know that he had learned his lesson at last! So many people laughed at him for posting his handkerchief that he didn't have a chance to forget his silliness, and now his brains are just as good as anyone else's!

The Poor Pink Pig

Once upon a time there was a fat pink pig who belonged to Mother Winkle. Mother Winkle was half a witch and she sometimes made spells, but she didn't really know very much about them, and so they often went wrong.

The pig was called Tubby, and Mother Winkle often used to call him into the kitchen to help her with her spells. She hadn't a green-eyed black cat to help her, as most witches have – she couldn't afford one, for they were very expensive to buy. But Tubby the pink pig did quite well instead.

Tubby hated having to help Mother Winkle. The spells smelled funny, and you never knew when green or yellow smoke would suddenly appear, or flames jump out of nothing. So he used to try to hide when he knew Mother Winkle was doing magic. It wasn't any good though – Mother Winkle always found him. He was too fat to hide himself properly.

One day Mother Winkle shooed him into the kitchen to help her to do a new spell. Someone had given her a spell for magic cakes, and she wanted to make some. But to do that she had to get Tubby to stand in the middle of a circle of chalk while she stood outside and sang a lot of magic words.

Tubby didn't want to help, but he had to. He stood there in the middle of the chalk circle, looking very fat and miserable. Mother Winkle stood outside with her magic stick and book, and then she began to recite enchanted words in a sing-song voice.

In two minutes, to Tubby's enormous surprise, a great many small currant cakes suddenly appeared inside the chalk circle, just by him.

There they were, smelling new-baked and most delicious. Tubby's mouth watered and his nose twitched. How he longed to sniff at one of those cakes, but he didn't dare move while the magic was going on.

Just as Mother Winkle put her book down to go and fetch a plate for the magic cakes, a knock came at the door.

"Bother! That's the butcher!" said Mother Winkle and went to the door, leaving Tubby and the cakes alone in the circle.

Well, that was too much for Tubby. As soon as Mother Winkle's back was turned

he sniffed at a cake, and it smelled so
good he ate it. My goodness me, it tasted
good too! Tubby ate another – and
another – and another! In fact, he had
eaten nearly all of them when Mother
Winkle came back!

And then Tubby noticed something
very, very strange. Mother Winkle looked
enormous! Simply *enormous*! He couldn't

make it out. He looked round the room – and squealed in surprise. The chairs and the tables were enormous too!

Those magic cakes had a spell in them to make anyone who ate them grow much smaller! Tubby had eaten a lot and he was now very tiny. Each cake had made him half his size!

Mother Winkle stared at him in amazement, and then she stamped her foot in anger.

"Oh, you silly, greedy stupid pig! You've eaten nearly all my magic cakes! You wicked creature! Wait till I make you your right size again, and I'll turn you into bacon!"

Tubby was so frightened that he leaped out of the chalk circle and ran into a corner. Mother Winkle ran after him – and then the little pig discovered that it was much easier to hide himself now he was tiny. He squeezed into a mouse-hole and stood quite still there. Mother Winkle poked here and there under the chairs but she couldn't find him anywhere.

Tubby squeezed himself still further back in the mouse-hole – and found himself against something warm and soft.

"Hello, hello!" said a squeaky voice. "Who are you?"

Tubby turned and saw a little brown mouse with bright black eyes.

"I hope I'm not in your way," he said politely. "But the truth is I'm trying to hide from that horrid person Mother Winkle. She is going to turn me into bacon."

"Dear, dear!" said the mouse, shaking his head in dismay. "I'm sorry for you, I really am. She is not a nice person. She is mean. She never leaves a single crumb out for me or my family. Why don't you run away?"

"That's a good idea!" said Tubby, in delight. "Why should I ever go back? Oh, but, Mouse – there's one thing I had forgotten – I'm too tiny. Who will make me a big, proper pig again, if I don't go back to Mother Winkle?"

"No one will," said the mouse cheerfully. "But why do you want to be a big, proper pig? It's much nicer to be small. I've been small all my life and it suits me very well. You can hide beautifully, and creep anywhere you like. I should keep small if I were you, Piggy-wig."

Tubby thought about it, and he decided that the mouse was right. It would be nice to be small.

"But I must find a home somewhere," he said to the mouse. "I must belong to someone."

"Well, creep through my hole," said the mouse. "I'll show you where it goes. It leads to a farm, and you can ask the farmer's wife if she will keep you for her own pig. She is very kind to all animals. I expect she will let you live on her farm."

So Tubby followed the kind little mouse through the long tunnel, and at last came up into a field. The mouse poked his head out to see if any of the cats were about, but none was to be seen.

"There's the farmer's wife, look!" whispered the mouse. "Feeding her chickens – do you see? Go and ask her now."

Tubby said goodbye to the mouse and hurried over to the farmer's wife. He squeaked at her from the ground and she suddenly saw him among her hens, looking very small indeed, tinier than the tiniest chick. She picked him up in astonishment.

"Will you give me a home?" squeaked Tubby. "I have run away, and I want a new home."

The farmer's wife laughed and shook her head.

"You funny little creature!" she said. "You wouldn't be any good to me! You're too small! The other pigs would gobble you up. No, no you must go somewhere else!"

Tubby scampered away. He was sad. Where should he go now? He wandered on and on and at last came to a hillside where sheep, looking as large as elephants, were all busily eating the grass.

"I'd like to live out here on the hillside," thought Tubby. "There's plenty of sunshine, and the sheep wouldn't take any notice of me. I'll go and ask the shepherd if he'll have me."

So he went to where the shepherd was sitting on the grass, looking at the sky to see if rain was coming.

"Will you have me for your own?" squeaked the pig to the surprised shepherd. "I'm a pig run away from home. I'm a real pig, but very small."

The shepherd threw back his head and laughed.

"Who wants a tiny pig like you!" he

said. "You're no use to anyone. My dogs would smell you out and nibble you. Go away while there's time."

The poor pink pig scampered off in a hurry, looking behind him to see if the sheepdogs were coming. He went on until he came to a goose-girl, taking her geese on to the common. He ran up to her and tugged at the lace in her shoe.

"Let me be your pig!" he squealed. "Let me live with your geese!"

The goose-girl looked at him in astonishment.

"But what use are you?" she asked. "Such a little thing as you are! Who wants a pig as tiny as you!"

The geese saw the tiny pig and began

to hiss and cackle. They crowded round Tubby and he was frightened. He slipped between their yellow legs and ran off as fast as he could.

He hid himself all day, afraid of cats, dogs and geese. When night came he set out once more, and soon came to a big house. He squeezed himself under the door and went in. The first room he came to was full of toys. There were dolls on a shelf, a ball on the floor, a clockwork engine in a cupboard with soldiers and a kite, and, just by the wall, a big Noah's ark.

Everyone was surprised to see the pink pig.

"Are you a toy?" asked the biggest doll.

"No, I'm a proper pig, but very small," said the pig.

He told the toys all his adventures, and they were sorry for him. All the animals in the Noah's ark came out to look at him. There were two elephants, two bears, two lions, two tigers, two cows, two goats, two chickens, two ducks – in fact, two of everything.

175

No – not quite two of everything, after all. There was only one pig, a little black one. He ran over to Tubby and had a good look at him.

"Oh!" he said. "I really thought at first that you were the other Noah's ark pig come back again. You know, he was left out of the ark one day, on the carpet – and when the housemaid swept up the next morning, she swept the little pig into her dust-pan, and we never saw him again."

"We think he must have been put into the dustbin with the rubbish and taken away," said the biggest doll, sadly. "We missed him very much. You are rather like him."

"I am very lonely without him," said the black Noah's ark pig. "I suppose, little live pig, you wouldn't like to be a toy pig and live with us in the ark? We have great fun, for the children often take us out and walk us all round the floor. You would be well taken care of too, and we would all be friends with you."

Well, you can imagine how delighted

Tubby was! He rubbed his nose against the black pig's nose and squealed for joy.

"Of course I'll live with you!" he cried. "I'd love to! I don't want to be big any more. I like being little. And oh, it will be such fun living with so many animals. But, little black pig, are you sure the lions and bears won't eat me?"

"Oh goodness me, no!" said the black pig. "They are made of wood. They are not alive like you. You will have to pretend to be made of wood too, when the children play with us."

"Oh, I can easily do that!" said Tubby. He climbed back into the ark with all the others, and settled down for the night. He was so pleased to have found such a nice home. The ark was warm and comfortable, and the other animals were friendly and jolly. He was very happy.

But when the children, Anne and Margaret, played with their Noah's ark animals next day, how surprised they were!

"Margaret! Here's another little pig instead of the one we lost!" cried Anne, picking up Tubby. "Oh, isn't he nice and fat! He looks so real too. I wonder who put him there."

Nobody knew. Mother didn't know, nor

did Father. Granny shook her head and so did Jane the housemaid. Nobody knew at all. You can't think how puzzled they all were!

Tubby still lives in the Noah's ark – and I'd love to tell Anne and Margaret how he got there, wouldn't you?

The
Squeaky Doll

There was once a tiny rubber doll, no bigger than your middle finger, who lived in Betsy-May's doll's-house. Betsy-May loved this doll because she could squeak. Whenever she was squeezed in her middle she said "Eee-eee", just like that.

But one day a dreadful thing happened to the rubber doll. Betsy-May took her out of the doll's-house to show her to Tommy, who had come to tea – and Tommy trod on her quite by accident.

And that killed the squeak in the poor little doll. She couldn't squeak any more at all. You can't think how sad she was, because, you see, it was the only voice she had.

There were three other dolls in the doll's-house – two tiny wooden ones and a little china one. They were very upset when the rubber doll lost her squeak.

"Let us put her to bed for a day," they said. "Maybe she will get her squeak back if she rests."

So they put her to bed in one of the little beds in the dolls' bedroom, and looked after her well. But when she got up again, she still had no squeak, though all the dolls pressed her as hard as they could in the middle.

Betsy-May was just as sad as the dolls about it. She looked at the little rubber doll and squeezed her in the middle – but no squeak came.

"I don't like you so much now," said Betsy-May. "You don't seem right without a squeak."

Well, that made the rubber doll cry bitterly that night. It was dreadful not to be liked so much. After all, she couldn't help losing her squeak. The other dolls comforted her, and gave her a tiny sweet out of the toy sweet-shop.

Then they put her to bed again, and tucked her up well. They went down into the kitchen and talked about the poor rubber doll.

"It would be so lovely to hear her squeak again," said the china doll, lighting a tiny candle in a candlestick, for it was dark in the dolls' kitchen.

And just at that very moment they heard a perfectly lovely squeak. "Eee-eee-eee!" it went. "Eee-eee-eee!"

"The rubber doll has got her squeak back!" they cried, and they rushed upstairs. But no – how odd – the rubber doll was fast asleep and not squeaking at all. As the three dolls stood looking down at her, they heard the squeak again. "Eee-eee-eee!"

And then somebody knocked quietly on the little knocker on the doll's-house front door. Down went the three dolls to see who it was.

Outside the door stood a tiny mouse. He twitched his fine whiskers and spoke humbly to the dolls.

"Oh, please, the clown told me you

wanted a squeak, and I have a fine one. I am very, very hungry, so if you would give me something to eat, I will let you have my squeak." The dolls stared in delight.

"Come in," said the china doll. "I hope we have got something for you to eat. But I don't believe we have, you know."

The mouse went in. The dolls opened the little kitchen cupboard – but it was quite, quite empty. There was nothing to eat at all!

"Oh dear, what a pity," said the china doll. "It would have been marvellous to have got a new squeak for the rubber doll."

The baby mouse looked at the candle burning on the table. "Could I have that candle to eat?" he asked. "It is made of tallow, and I like tallow."

"Goodness gracious! Fancy wanting to eat a candle!" cried the dolls. They blew it out at once, took it from the tiny candlestick and gave it to the mouse. He asked them for a glass of water. When they gave it to him he squeaked into it

about twenty times. Then he put his paw over the top of the glass and gave it to the china doll.

"Let the rubber doll drink this and her squeak will come back," he said. Then off he went out of the front door with his candle. What a treat for him!

The three dolls rushed upstairs and

woke the surprised rubber doll. They made her drink the glass of water. Then they pressed her hard in the middle. "EEEE-EEEE-EEEE!" she said, just like that. Wasn't she surprised!

"Oh, your squeak is back again!" cried the china doll. "Won't Betsy-May be pleased?"

Well, Betsy-May was pleased, of course, but she could never imagine where the little candle in the doll's-house had gone. You could tell her, couldn't you?

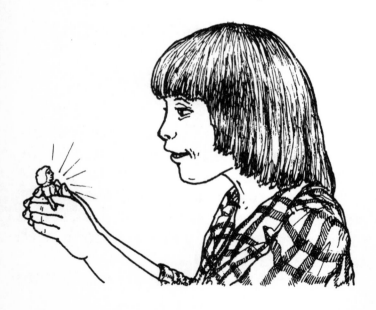

The
Grumpy Goblins

Alan was cross and tired. He had worked hard at school all day, and then when he had got home to tea, his mother had sent him out on errands until bedtime.

"I haven't done my homework!" said Alan to his mother, when she said it was time for bed.

"Well, what homework is it?" she asked.

"I've got to think of twelve words beginning with *gr*," said Alan. "Miss Brown says the *gr* family is quite easy, and we must all come to school tomorrow ready to make sentences with words beginning with those two letters. So, Mum, I must sit down and think some out."

"Oh, you can do that in bed!" said his

187

mother, and Alan had to go upstairs at once. He was cross because he felt sure it would be difficult to think out homework in bed – and he was right, for no sooner was he under the bedclothes, trying to think, than his mind wandered away and wouldn't even try to get hold of any *gr* words.

"If only somebody would tell me a few!" thought the little boy. He opened his eyes – and how he stared! What do you think he saw? He saw six funny little goblins round on his bed, and one of them was holding a dog on a lead. The dog was just like Alan's own toy dog, but he seemed to be very much alive.

"Who are you?" asked Alan, sitting up.

"We're the Grumpy Goblins," said one.

"Oh," said Alan, "I suppose you are always cross then."

"We grumble," said one.

"And we groan," said another.

"And we grouse," said the third.

"And we growl," said the dog, unexpectedly, and gave a fierce growl that made Alan jump. Then the dog

jumped up on to the bed, but the goblin
pulled him back.

"Grab him!" said the others.

"He wants one of my chocolates!" said
Alan, seeing the little dog sniffing in the
direction of his box of sweets.

"Greedy dog!" said the goblin who had
the dog's lead.

"Grubby fellow!" said another. The dog jumped back on to the foot of the bed with a grunt.

"He grunts like a pig," said the first goblin.

"Gracious!" said the dog's master. "Now he's grinning!" Sure enough the dog was smiling from ear to ear. Alan thought it was all most interesting.

"Do tell me why you've come to visit me," said Alan.

"Your grievance called us," said the goblins. "Though gruff and grumpy and grave, we granted your wish."

"What wish?" Alan asked sleepily.

"Well! Where's your gratitude?" snapped the goblin. "Come, Grumpies – and gradually – gradually – gracefully – gracefully . . ."

"Gradually gracefully what?" said Alan, half-asleep – but the Grumpy Goblins were gone! The dog jumped on to the bed and snuggled beside Alan. The little boy slept.

When he awoke in the morning he looked at the dog and remembered the strange goblins. "You are my own toy dog, after all!" he said. "I wonder what you were doing with those goblins. Oh – I think I know – you fetched them to do my homework for me. Yes – they did it all! I can write down heaps of words beginning with *gr* this morning – and I bet I'll get top marks!"

He did. Could you?